MIK AND THE PROWLER

Mik and the Prowler

YOSHIKO UCHIDA

Illustrated by William M. Hutchinson

HOUGHTON MIFFLIN COMPANY

BOSTON

Atlanta   Dallas   Geneva, Illinois

Palo Alto   Princeton   Toronto

ISBN 0-395-61816-9

3456789-B-96 95 94 93

For Wasa Oba San

PREFACE

It's not often that an author has the opportunity to bring an old book back to life after so many years, and I'm delighted that MIK AND THE PROWLER is available again to a new generation of readers.

If I were writing this book today, however, I might have written it quite differently, for the world has changed a great deal and so have I. Perhaps I might have made Mik's father an engineer or a lawyer or maybe even an astronaut because Japanese Americans could be and are any of these.

At the time I wrote MIK AND THE PROWLER, however, many doors were still closed to Japanese Americans, and gardening, considered by some to be a demeaning occupation, was often the only job they could find. I wanted to show that it was (and still is) an honorable and respectable occupation in which intelligent, caring men such as Mik's father could own their own businesses. I also wanted to emphasize, as I try to do in all my books, that we all need to respect one another for who we are, not for the kind of work we do.

I hope this book will be read with an understanding of the times in which it was written, and not be judged solely in terms of the awareness we have achieved today.

Y. U.

September 1991

CONTENTS

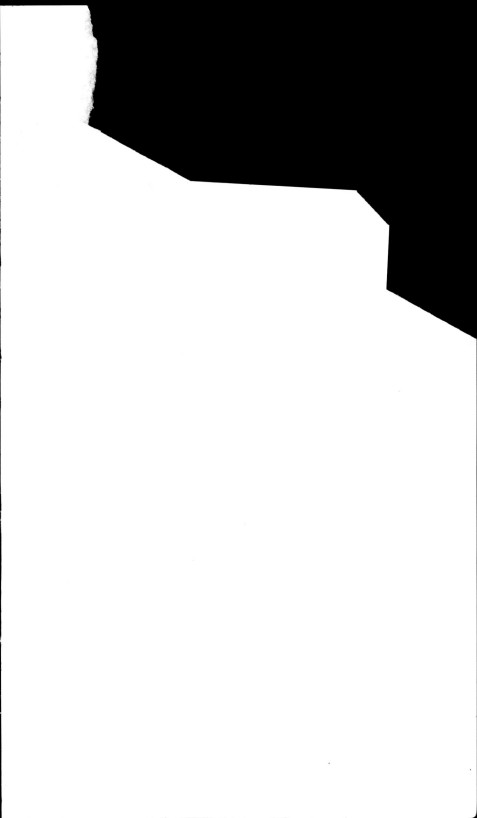

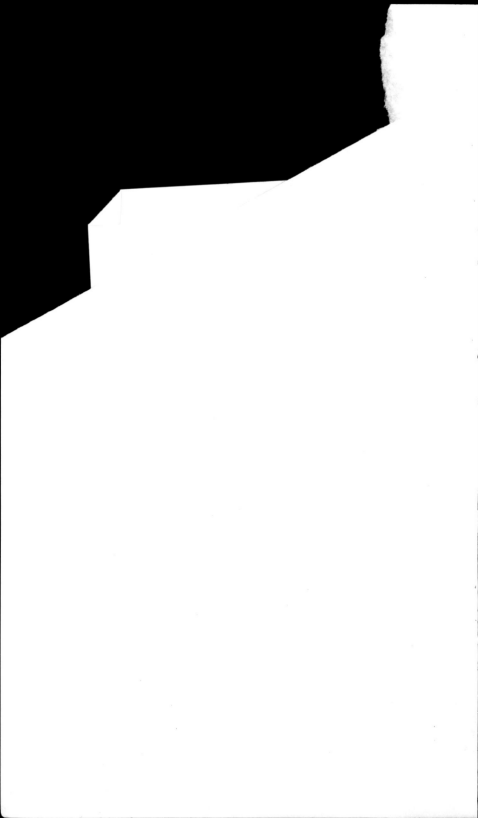

CHAPTER 1

A Job for Mrs. Whipple

Mik darted up the steps of Mrs. Whipple's lavender house two at a time and then slowed down as he heard the warning clink of the custard cups he carried in Mom's wicker basket.

"Oh, oh," he said to himself.

The last thing his mother had said as he started for Mrs. Whipple's was, "Be careful, Mik. Don't tilt the basket."

Mik looked inside the basket and saw that the custard slanted like the deck of a carrier in a gale. "Oh, oh," he murmured again, and quickly threw the checkered cloth back over it. The smell of nutmeg drifted from the basket, and Mik swallowed hard. He gave the bell five quick rings so Mrs. Whipple would be sure to hear.

She heard, of course, and hurried to the door, her gray hair flying in short curly wisps around her plump face.

"Why, Mikitaro Watanabe," she said. She always liked to say his full Japanese name in just that way, because she thought it was so musical. "It must have been mental tele-pathy," she continued. "I was just thinking of you and wish-ing you would come, and here you are, just the person who can help me out!"

Mik grinned and thrust the basket toward her.

"Mom made some baked custard for you since you can't chew," he announced, as though Mrs. Whipple hadn't a tooth in her mouth.

Actually, Mik's mother had sent it over because she knew Mrs. Whipple had had two wisdom teeth extracted, and also because she was a good friend. She was, in fact, one of Mik's very special friends. When he had gone around the neighborhood last year to get "starts" for the *Herald,* she was the only one who had invited him inside. Furthermore, she had even offered him a cup of cocoa. Mik knew then that Mrs. Whipple was special. She was A-1, a "good guy."

"Come in, come in," Mrs. Whipple urged. "Find a place to sit down."

This was never very simple to do in her house, because Mrs. Whipple was a maker of hooked rugs and had small piles of colored wool and yarn heaped on every chair in the living room and over most of the floor as well. It was as though a family of moles had come through her house and dug up mounds of wool all over her carpet.

Just as Mik found a spot where he could sit down, Mrs. Whipple appeared with an enormous slice of homemade gingerbread. It was covered with a great flowing glob of whipped cream, and it smelled so good it made Mik feel weak in the knees. Mrs. Whipple knew exactly what was important in life.

"Conversation flows much more smoothly over a good slice of homemade cake," she always said, and Mik knew she was absolutely right. He'd had some of the best conversations in his life over Mrs. Whipple's chocolate cakes or her gingerbread baked with slivers of fresh gingerroot.

"Now, this is my problem," Mrs. Whipple said, as though she had been saving up those very words to say to Mik the moment she had given him a slice of her gingerbread. "I am going to visit my nephew Clarence in Monterey next week."

Mik was in no position to comment. His mouth was full, and he could only nod as Mrs. Whipple went on.

"I'll need someone to water the garden and feed Cassandra and Fredericka for me," Mrs. Whipple continued. Cassandra and Fredericka were Mrs. Whipple's two Siamese cats and all the family she had. She was a widow and lived all alone. The neighbors hadn't known this when she moved in, and so it was a source of great puzzlement to them when she would step out on the porch to call Fredericka.

"Fred! Oh, Freddie!" she would call in a high voice that floated through the dusky air past half the houses on the block. Naturally, everyone thought she was calling her husband.

"My, he must be a trial," the neighbors said to one another, and they clucked their tongues sympathetically.

Since Mik considered Mrs. Whipple an A-1, white hat, special friend, he thought it was his duty to give the neighbors the true facts. "Mrs. Whipple is a widow," he would explain patiently, "and Freddie is her cat." Then the neighbors would smile and look as though they had just found the missing word in a crossword puzzle. "Ah," they would say, "so she is a widow," and they showered her with invitations to luncheon and to tea.

"Would you be willing to do it for me for two weeks?" Mrs. Whipple asked now, continuing with the words she had saved up for Mik. "You're the very first person I thought of, because you're so dependable."

"Sure," Mik answered quickly.

No one at home ever told him he was dependable. In fact, he was getting a pretty miserable reputation, because he could never remember the things he was told to do. Just last week, for instance, he had ridden his bike again at night without lights, and, naturally, he had gotten a ticket. He had not only gotten a ticket, he'd had to go to court at the City Hall, and he didn't get one drop of sympathy from anybody at home. Dad had been telling him for weeks that he should either buy lights or stop riding his bike at night, and Mom had told him he had to learn to be more responsible.

Now, here was Mrs. Whipple asking him to take care of her beautiful garden—the prettiest one on the whole block— and to feed her precious Siamese cats. That was being about as responsible as he could get. Wait till Mom and Dad heard that!

"Sure I will," Mik said again to Mrs. Whipple. Summer vacation had just begun, and there was still a month before he went to Y Camp. (That is, if he sold enough Y soap to pay for half his way. That was the agreement he had made with Dad.)

"I'll get Corky to help me," Mik continued. Corky Hunter was one of his best friends. Like Mik, he was ten and in the fifth grade at school. He lived just a few houses away, which made it very convenient, since he and Mik did just about everything together.

Mik knew, in fact, that Corky was exactly the right person to help him. Corky was a very responsible fellow. He never forgot things. He always bought everything on his mother's grocery list and didn't have to run back, as Mik often did, to buy some thyme or parsley or something else that was written on the back of the list. Corky always turned in his book reports on time, and he never got caught riding his bike at night without lights. He would surely help Mik remember to keep Mrs. Whipple's lawn green and her cats fed.

"I'll leave you the key to my back door," Mrs. Whipple went on, spreading her plan before him like a map on which he could trace his course. "And I'll leave cat food in the cupboard and some milk in the refrigerator."

Suddenly Mrs. Whipple stopped, and her face crinkled up in a frown. "Oh dear," she said. "What shall we do about Mr. Potts?"

Mr. Potts was the man next door. He was lame and cranky, and he hated cats. He had a small aviary in his back yard, which he loved dearly. It contained one ring-necked pheasant, Mathilda; one dove, Sarah; and two parakeets, Gladys and Henry. Furthermore, he considered every cat he ever saw a personal enemy. He and Mrs. Whipple weren't exactly enemies, but they weren't exactly friends either.

Mr. Potts told Mrs. Whipple that her cats always sat on the fence looking at his birds like two housewives examining some good T-bone steaks.

"I don't trust them," he would say, with a big scowl on his face.

But Mrs. Whipple would answer sweetly, "Nonsense. My Cassie and Freddie would never touch your birds."

Nevertheless, in order to keep peace over their ivy-covered fence, Mrs. Whipple bought little red collars with bells on them and was careful to put them on the cats whenever she let them out.

"Aw, I'm not afraid of Mr. Potts," Mik said boldly.

As a matter of fact, he scarcely knew him, because Mr. Potts spent most of his time sitting inside his dark, dismal house.

"Besides," Mik went on, "I'll never forget to bell the cats when I let them out."

"Good boy!" Mrs. Whipple said, smiling. "I knew I could count on you."

And so it was all settled. Mrs. Whipple would leave on Saturday and give her key to Mik on Friday. Furthermore, Mrs. Whipple said she would like to give Mik fifty cents a day for his troubles. "Reimburse," was the way she put it. In two weeks' time he'd earn seven dollars, and with that and the money he'd have from selling the rest of his Y soap,

Mik figured he could easily earn half his way to summer camp.

All the way home Mik thought of Camp Mohala and the cold blue lake up in the Sierras. He thought of the night-time sings around the campfire and of the stars that looked like pinpricks of light in the dark sky. He could almost smell the pine trees and the bacon that sizzled over an early morning campfire on overnight hikes. And suddenly, he couldn't keep his feet from running. He raced home, his heart singing.

Dad's truck pulled up in front of the house just as he got home. Dad didn't get home until pretty late these days, because summer was always the busiest time of year for him. In fact, Dad was busy all year long because so many people wanted him to work on their gardens. Mik knew Dad was just about the best gardener in town. Everybody said so, including Mom, who said he could make sweet peas bloom on the granite boulders of Yosemite if he wanted to. Mik was pretty proud of him, all right. Pictures of his gardens were always turning up in the House and Garden section of the Sunday paper, and he won all kinds of ribbons at the annual garden show in the auditorium.

"Hi," he called to Mik now. His face was brown from long days in the sun, and his shoes were covered with dust. He looked tired, but it wasn't a cross-tired look. Dad always said it was different to be tired from working in the sun and fresh air. It wasn't like being tired from shuffling too many papers on a desk.

"Guess we'd better go in the back way, or we'll hear from your mother," he said as he brushed off his shirt.

Mik didn't even wait to get into the house. "I have a job with Mrs. Whipple," he said, telling just what he would be doing while she went to Monterey. "That's being pretty responsible, huh, Dad?" he asked.

"It surely is, Mik," Dad said. "It's a big trust, and I hope you can do it." It was as though Mik had just told him he had been appointed vice-president of a bank.

Mom was just as pleased. "Why, that's wonderful, Mik," she said. "It will be a fine responsibility for you."

Only his big brother, Bud, wasn't very enthusiastic. Bud was fourteen and thought he knew everything. "Better watch out for old man Potts," he warned. "He's a cat hater from way back."

"Aw, he doesn't scare me," Mik said. But deep down he felt a tiny twinge of worry sneaking toward the pit of his stomach. "I can handle him," he added, but he said it more to convince himself than Bud.

Mik's little brother, Pete, suddenly popped out from beneath the table, where he had been looking for fleas on Bowser. Bowser was Mik's pet shepherd collie, and Pete knew he was the best dog in the whole United States. After all, he had been told a number of times that it was Bowser, good old Bowser, who had rescued him, wet and dripping, from an irrigation ditch that he fell into when he was two. Pete was almost four now, but he still remembered about the ditch, and he made it his special mission in life to help Bowser relieve himself of fleas.

"Watch out for Mr. Potts," Pete said now, copying Bud.

"Aw, for Pete's sake," Mik said, and then he was immediately sorry. Whenever anyone said that, Pete thought he was being talked to.

"What say?" he asked Mik now, pulling at his sleeve. "What say?"

"I said who wants to buy some Y soap?" Mik answered.

But neither Pete nor Mother nor anyone else seemed to be listening. Mik really didn't feel much like selling soap now anyway. He was still thinking about Mr. Potts and wondering if he might be mean enough to harm Cassie and Freddie while Mrs. Whipple was away. After all, people did say he didn't have a friend in the world, and they probably said it for a good reason.

CHAPTER 2

Pete's Wild Ride

Friday morning Mik was up even before Pete, which was pretty early, since Pete usually liked to get up at six-thirty and wake up the whole house. Mik had a feeling something exciting might happen. He leaped out of bed as though there were a mountain lake waiting for him just a few feet away. There wasn't, though. There was only a heap of clothes—Bud's clothes—which had been left on the floor all night.

Mik looked at Bud still asleep in the upper bunk, his nose squashed against the pillow. He had half a notion to throw a wet towel on his face, but he remembered how angry Bud had been the last time he did that. He had pinned Mik to the floor and made him say "uncle." Besides, Bud was different these days. He cleaned his fingernails, combed his hair, and wore white shirts when he went out. He was acting pretty peculiar. No, Mik decided, no towel for Bud. Instead he raced downstairs and discovered that Mom was cooking oatmeal. The sun was pouring through the kitchen window like a bucketful of butter.

"Zingies," Mik said. "What a day for a picnic!"

"I should say," Mom replied. "No fog, no smog. It'd be perfect."

Dad was sitting at the table reading his paper, but he hadn't missed the point of the little conversation at all. Ever since summer vacation had started, they'd all been trying to make him take a day off, but every day he said he was too busy.

"What a day for work, you mean," he said. "With all this hot sun, my gardens are either drying up or have grass two inches high that needs to be cut. What I need is a good assistant."

"What about me?" Mik asked immediately. This wasn't the first time he had offered his help. In fact, he had offered it a number of times before, but Dad had said no. Somehow, he didn't seem to have any faith in Mik since the time Mik had left the hose turned on at the Horlichs'. That was a pretty terrible thing to do, especially since that happened to be the week the Horlichs were away on vacation. The neighbors called Dad to tell him someone had forgotten to turn off the water, and the patio had been flooded.

"I wouldn't forget to turn off the water anyplace," Mik said now.

But Mom reminded him of the job at Mrs. Whipple's. "It's better to have one job and to do it well," she said. "Besides, I want you to watch Petey for me this afternoon."

Mik groaned. "Aw, I always have to watch Pete," he complained. "Why can't Bud do it?"

"Bud's got too much on his mind," Mother answered absently.

As if Mik didn't. There was Bowser, who needed badly to be wormed. There was also Carmichael, his pet parrot (given to him by Mr. Monroney, the ice-cream man). Carmichael needed more lessons in whistling. It was really very difficult to try to teach a parrot where to put his tongue. And finally, there was Mrs. Whipple. He'd have to go over and get her key this afternoon.

"I have an awful lot on my mind too, Mom," Mik said.

But Mom wasn't impressed at all. She was asking Dad what he thought Grandma Watanabe would like for her birthday.

"Sure, that'd be fine," he said, his nose in the sports page. He didn't have the vaguest notion what Mom had said.

Mom didn't listen to Mik, and Dad didn't listen to Mom. Nobody listens to anybody around here, Mik thought.

"Well, Helen, I'm off," Dad said, finishing his coffee. "We'll have a picnic someday when I'm caught up with the gardens. All right?"

"I know," Mom answered. "Some nice rainy, soggy day when you can't work."

Dad grinned and kissed her good-by. "Tell Bud he may be drafted as an assistant one of these days," he said, and he was gone.

It looked to Mik as though it might be a pretty dull day.

"I think I may get a nice drip-dry blouse for your grand-ma," Mom said later, as she prepared to leave. Then she re-minded Mik to be careful. "Do try to be responsible and remember you're watching Petey," she cautioned.

Mik nodded. The last time he had stayed home with his little brother, he was so busy working on a Geiger counter with Corky that he'd forgotten all about Pete. By the time he discovered him, Pete had eaten two bananas, a small package of sugar-coated corn flakes, and half a box of pret-zels. Not only that, he had opened two brand-new packages of corn chips and cheese crackers and spilled them all over the kitchen floor. Bowser, of course, had a great time help-ing Petey eat. The two of them had had quite a picnic. When Mom got home, however, it was Mik who got most of the scolding. "After all," she said, "you were responsible for watching Petey."

Things would be different today, Mik thought as he lis-tened to his mother. He would have to be very responsible at Mrs. Whipple's, and he was going to begin today.

"O.K., Mom. O.K.," he said. "I'll be the most responsi-blest baby sitter you ever had. You watch."

"Just keep Petey off the streets," she said, and then she waved and drove off in the station wagon.

The minute she was gone, Pete made his usual little an-nouncement. "Ice cream," he demanded.

Mik had made the mistake of buying him an ice-cream bar from Mr. Monroney one day when he stayed home with him, and ever since, he tried asking for ice cream at least once.

"I want ice cream," Pete said again.

Mik was firm. "No ice cream," he said, "and that's final!"

Exactly at that moment, Mik heard the bells of Mr. Monroney's ice-cream cart. It was a small white cart with a row of bells strung along the handle, which Mr. Monroney jingled as he walked. Each summer he went up and down the streets of Berkeley, wearing a spanking white jacket, a black bow tie, and a pair of brown trousers. He also had an old brown hat with a small red feather thrust in its band.

"This is my good-luck hat," Mr. Monroney explained, and he was never without it. The strange thing, however, was that he kept it on top of his cart instead of on his head, as though he thought that was a nice polite way for a cart to look. There was a picture of an orange popsicle painted on the side of the cart, and just under the row of bells was a piece of cardboard with his name on it. "Percival H. Monroney," it read, and it was stuck to the cart with a piece of Scotch tape.

"Hello, Mik," he called now.

He didn't ask if Mik would like an ice-cream bar. As a matter of fact, he never seemed to care whether he sold any ice cream or not.

"I just enjoy walking in the fresh air and making people happy," he always said. "And ice cream makes people just about as happy as anything I know. That's why I like this job. Besides," he would add, "I learn a lot from walking up and down the streets and talking to people. Take your father, for instance," he would say to Mik. "I've learned more about plants and growing things from him than I would from a dozen books."

Just as Mr. Monroney came up with his cart, Petey began to cry. He was pretty spoiled, being the youngest, and he still thought crying would get him what he wanted. The trouble was that it sometimes did.

It pained Mr. Monroney to see children cry. He looked troubled, and he tugged at his big brown mustache.

"Say," he said. "I'll give you a ride on my cart, Pete, old man." And he lifted Petey on top of his cart, jiggled his bells, and pushed the cart along. Of course, Pete stopped crying immediately. He straddled the cart like a horse and shouted, "Giddap."

If the little girl across the street hadn't called for an orange popsicle just then, Pete probably never would have had his wild ride. She did, however, and so he did.

Mr. Monroney went across the street to give it to her, and that was when Pete shouted, "Giddap, Mik!" Just to be obliging, Mik gave the cart a really good push, and the cart began to roll. Mik had never thought of his street as being on a slope, but he found out then. He most surely did. He had just turned his head for a second to watch Mr. Monroney when the cart got away. The next thing Mik knew, it was headed straight for the corner intersection with the traffic lights. As it rolled on, it gained speed, and there was old Pete sitting on top of the cart, waving Mr. Monroney's brown hat and shouting at the top of his voice. It was really quite a sight.

Mik and Mr. Monroney ran after the cart, shouting frantically for it to stop. But, of course, there was no way in the world for Pete to stop the cart. As it sailed toward the intersection, Mik saw the lights change. All those cars would soon ram right into poor old Pete. Mik heard the horrible screech of brakes, and he had to close his eyes. When he opened them, there was Pete still sitting on top of the cart, right in the middle of the street. Cars were stopped all around him, honking their horns like mad.

Mik suddenly felt as though his legs were made of jelly, and he sat down on the curb. Good old Mr. Monroney, however, was right in the middle of everything. He ran to Petey and held up his hands to stop the cars. Then he pulled the cart back with one hand while he waved his good-luck hat with the other. Mik could see that it was surely a handy thing to have around for an emergency like this one.

"Big long ride," Pete gurgled happily as Mr. Monroney pulled up beside Mik and sat down.

"Whew," Mr. Monroney said. His face had turned a sort of purplish red, and he couldn't seem to squeeze out any words except "Hot socks, that was close!" and "Crispies! No more rides on the cart for you, young man."

Then, when he was completely out of words, he got up, wiped his forehead with a big blue handkerchief, and said he was leaving before anything else happened.

Corky came by just as the excitement had died down. When he heard what had happened, he whistled through his teeth. "Boy, it's a good thing all that ice cream got saved," he said. He was practical. He thought of things like that.

"I'll say," Mik agreed. He could be pretty practical too, especially about things like ice cream.

The two of them hurried Pete back home before Mom arrived and put him to work building a space ship with some old cartons. By the time Mom got home, everything was as calm as a lake in June.

"Everything all right?" she asked.

"Uh-huh," Mik said, but he didn't dare look her in the eye. She could tell in a minute when he wasn't telling the honest-to-goodness truth. He decided it was a good time to get Mrs. Whipple's key. "Got to go see Mrs. Whipple," he said, and he hurried off before Mom could ask any more questions.

As Mik walked up the street, he bumped into Clancy Berryman. Clancy lived two blocks from Mrs. Whipple and was a monster ogre—a bad guy. He was twelve, tough, and a good head taller than Mik. Everybody knew what a mean thing he'd done to the younger newsboys the time they all went to the State Fair in Sacramento. He had made each of them give him five cents of their spending money so he and the bigger boys could buy extra hot dogs. He had taken money from Mik then, too. No one liked him at school, either, and he spent more time in the principal's office than anyone else Mik knew.

Clancy grinned at Mik now. "Almost lost your kid brother today, dincha?" he asked.

Even Clancy knew about Petey's ride. A fine start Mik had made at being responsible. If Mrs. Whipple knew what had happened today, she'd probably never trust Mik with her precious cats.

Mik picked up a pebble and threw it hard at the telephone pole. It missed by a good two inches.

"Darn it," Mik muttered darkly. He felt as though he couldn't do anything right.

CHAPTER 3

The Hungry Prowler

When Mik arrived at Mrs. Whipple's house, he found it as neat as a brand-new pair of shoes. It was as though a giant vacuum cleaner had whooshed through, picking up the heaps of wool, the old slippers Cassie and Freddie played with, and all the scraps of paper on which Mrs. Whipple wrote recipes and notes to herself. Mik had never seen the house so tidy. All the house plants were gathered at the sink for watering, and already the shades throughout the house were half drawn.

Mrs. Whipple got right down to business without even a delay for cookies or milk. It wasn't often she did that.

"Here are the cans of Dr. Pepper's Pet Pepper," she said, opening the cupboard to show Mik. There were enough wavering stacks of cans piled from the floor to last until Christmas.

"And here," she continued, opening the refrigerator, "are two cartons of milk and some lamb's liver from **Mr.**

Putnam's. I'll leave you money for more milk when you need it."

Mik nodded and tried to look dependable as Mrs. Whipple led him on a tour of the house.

"This is the Imari china set my dear father brought back from Japan," she explained as she suddenly got the notion to show Mik her china closet. "And here are the ship models Captain Whipple made while he was at sea."

She reached toward the top shelf, poking about for fascinating objects that might interest Mik. "Look at this, Mikitaro," she said, holding up a row of carved-ivory elephants marching on a teakwood base. "This came from Hong Kong, I think."

Then, suddenly, she seemed to realize all this had nothing whatsoever to do with feeding Cassie and Freddie. After all, Mik wasn't going to be a house guest while she was gone.

"Why, we don't have to look at all this now," she said, and she went to an enormous roll-top desk in the corner of the dining room, swooshed back the top, and opened a secret drawer from which she produced a key. Then she shuffled through the papers scattered over the green blotter and handed Mik a list of the things she wanted him to do. At the very bottom Mik could see that she had printed something in large letters.

"Please be sure to lock the door when you leave the house, and please do not fail to bell the cats before you let them out." She had underlined almost every word.

Mik could tell by the way Mrs. Whipple repeated things

that she was a little worried. She had the same anxious look Mother had when she and Dad went out for the evening, leaving Mik and Bud to look after Pete. "Be careful, now," she'd say, and she would look as though she'd almost rather stay home than leave them alone.

Mrs. Whipple looked a little that way now, and Mik felt that he should say something reassuring. "You can count on me," he said firmly. "I'm very reliable."

Mrs. Whipple managed a smile then and said, "Of course you are. I trust you completely. I know Cassie and Freddie couldn't be in better hands."

Then she stood on the porch and waved until Mik reached the corner. He went home clutching the key in his hand and feeling tremendously responsible.

The next morning at ten o'clock Mik and Corky were already at Mrs. Whipple's watering her garden. Mik was careful to water at the roots and not over the heads of the plants. That was one of the first things Dad had taught him. He could also tell from what Dad had said that Mrs. Whipple's garden was well cared for and loved. The soil was rich and moist, and the plants were green-leafed and fresh. Even Mik could tell they'd had just the right amounts of sun, water, and food.

When the garden was watered, there was nothing more to do until four o'clock, when the cats were to be let out. Mik and Corky glanced over the fence, but Mr. Potts was nowhere in sight. His birds were roosting quietly in their aviary, and his house looked peaceful and serene. They decided it would be safe to leave.

By three-thirty, Mik and Corky were back. They belled the cats, looked out to see if Mr. Potts was around, and then let them out. Mik opened a can of Dr. Pepper's Pet Pepper and then looked for the liver. It wasn't there. Mik even remembered the pink butcher-paper it was wrapped in.

"Hey," he said, "the liver's gone."

He checked each shelf. There was butter, a jar of marmalade, half a loaf of raisin bread, and some cooky dough wrapped in a piece of plastic. But there was no liver.

"Maybe Mrs. Whipple ate it before she left," Corky suggested.

Mik shrugged. "That's funny," he said. "She told me to give it to the cats tonight."

When Cassie and Fred came home, however, they didn't seem to mind at all not having any liver. They ate the Pet Pepper as though it were a pound of round steak, and then they let Mik lock them up again in the house for the night. The job was going to be simple, Mik thought, and he and Corky went home whistling.

After four days, Mik knew that he had everything under control. The cats were behaving like well-brought-up children, Mr. Potts hadn't so much as shown his nose, and the garden almost looked like one of Dad's. Mik was being as responsible as a schoolteacher.

"Mrs. Whipple might like to hear from you," Mom suggested, and so Mik wrote her a letter.

"Cassie and Freddie are behaving fine," he wrote, "and I haven't forgot their bells once. Mr. Potts hasn't come after them or me—yet. I couldn't find the liver you left, but I'm fine. Petey chipped his front tooth when he fell off the porch (ours, not yours). I went swimming at the Y pool with Corky yesterday who is helping me water the lawn. Everything is fine. Your friend, Mikitaro Watanabe."

Mik mailed the letter on the way to Mrs. Whipple's house the next day, and that, he told himself later, was the biggest mistake he'd made. If only he hadn't written to tell her everything was fine, because when he got to her house, everything was about as unfine as it could possibly be. In the first place, when Mik and Corky opened the door, Cass and Fred didn't come leaping toward them, mewing and rubbing against their legs as they usually did.

"Hey, Cassie! Freddie!" Mik called, but the house was as still as the bottom of a well.

"Maybe they're hiding under the bed," Corky suggested. They went to the bedroom to see, and that was when they saw the open window. It was open just wide enough for the cats to squeeze out—without their bells!

"Did you open the window yesterday?" Mik asked, hoping Corky would say yes. But Corky shook his head so hard that his round fat cheeks quivered. "Heck, no," he protested. "Heck, no!"

"Then who did?"

"Maybe Mrs. Whipple's back," Corky suggested hopefully, but they both knew very well that she was still in Monterey. In fact, in another day she would be reading Mik's letter, telling her that everything was fine. "Good boy, Mikitaro," she would say as she read the letter. "I knew I could count on you."

Mik felt sick. "If it wasn't you or me," he asked slowly, "who opened the window?"

It was bad enough knowing that Cassie and Freddie had gotten out without their bells, but it was almost worse to think someone had sneaked into Mrs. Whipple's neat little house and left the window open on the way out. Or *was* he out?

Corky's gray eyes were wide and dark. "Maybe . . . maybe somebody's still in here," he said in a squeaky voice. If his hair hadn't been clipped so short, it would surely have stood on end. So would Mik's.

Mik felt goose-bumps pop out along his arms and the back of his neck. He wished he had a baseball bat to clobber the prowler with. He swallowed and tried to sound brave.

"Aw," he began. "Aw . . . nobody's here . . ."

But at that very moment there was a terrible banging at the back door. Then a voice shouted, "Say, you in there!"

Mik and Corky very nearly jumped out of their skins. Before they could run for the door, there was Mr. Potts standing in front of them, glaring like an angry lion.

"They've done it!" he shrieked at Mik. "Those miserable cats have torn off the door to my aviary and eaten Mathilda and Gladys and Henry. They're gone! All but Sarah, and it's a wonder they didn't eat her." Then he turned to glare at Mik. "And you. I hold you responsible. You were asked to watch those cats and see that they were properly belled."

Mr. Potts's glasses had slid halfway down his nose, and the thin strands of hair on his bald head were mussed like pieces of old straw.

"But I . . . they . . . the cats didn't do it," Mik sputtered hopelessly.

"Somebody broke into the house and let them out," Corky said, trying to say something helpful.

Mr. Potts, however, was angrier than a wet hornet. "Well, if the cats didn't do it, who did?" he shouted. "Look at them sitting on the porch, licking their chops as though they'd just eaten the best meal of their lives!"

"They're on the back porch?" Mik asked. "They're O.K.?"

He brushed past Mr. Potts with Corky at his heels. Mik couldn't think about Mr. Potts's birds now. He threw open the back door, and sure enough, there sat Cassie and Fred, just as prim as you please, cleaning themselves with quick licks of their small pink tongues. They did look satisfied and not very hungry. Had they really eaten the birds then? A flicker of doubt raced through Mik's mind, and for a terrible moment he wondered if Mr. Potts was right.

Mr. Potts was at his side now. "Look at them," he snarled. "They have 'guilty' written all over their faces. I shall see that they are sent to the pound and destroyed!"

Mik felt his heart turn to stone. "No!" he shouted. "Wait, Mr. Potts. I'll pay for the birds. I'll buy you some more. I'll make up for it."

But Mr. Potts simply turned away and lumbered down the steps. He wouldn't listen to anybody and muttered something about suing Mrs. Whipple.

"What an old grouch!" Corky growled.

"What a mess!" Mik groaned.

A fine reliable cat-sitter he'd turned out to be. He had let the cats out without bells, they had eaten Mr. Potts's birds—

maybe—and furthermore, he had even let a prowler get into Mrs. Whipple's house. What more could go wrong?

All the while, Mik kept thinking of Mrs. Whipple's smiling face as she read his letter. "Good for you, Mik," she was probably saying. "I knew I could count on you."

Mik wanted to dig a hole, crawl into it, and stay for a hundred years.

CHAPTER 4

Mr. Monroney's Good-Luck Hat

"Don't worry, Mik. I'm sure Mrs. Whipple will under-stand," Mom said as Mik blurted out the whole sad story at home.

"You really couldn't help it if someone broke in," Dad added. "After all, Mrs. Whipple didn't expect you to sit on her steps all day and guard her house."

"That was a pretty sneaky thing to do, all right," Bud said. "Wonder who knew Mrs. Whipple wasn't home?"

"I shoot him!" Pete yelled, pulling his water pistol from his cowboy holster for the twentieth time that day. "I shoot him!"

Even Bowser wagged his tail and licked Mik's hand sym-pathetically. Everybody realized what a terrible thing it was that had happened to Mik.

Mik couldn't eat his supper that night. He drank a glass of milk and ate a piece of bread, but even Mom's stew with dumplings didn't taste very good to him. He couldn't help but remember what Mr. Potts had said about sending Cassie and Freddie to the pound.

When supper was over, Dad said, "Well, let's go have a look. If anything's missing, we should notify the police."

Mom didn't even wash the dishes. "They can wait," she said, and she took off her apron, washed Pete's face, and hustled everybody into the station wagon. Even Bowser came along. Everyone went except Carmichael who, of course, had to stay home.

"Hello, boy, *sayonara, dasvedanya,*" he said sadly.

They picked up Corky, because he was all mixed up in this too, and then they marched into Mrs. Whipple's house like a crew from Scotland Yard. If a prowler had been lurking about, he certainly would have thought twice before trying to face that determined-looking collection of people and a dog.

Mik was the first to go in and the first to see the kitchen table.

"Holy mackerel!" he shouted. "Look at that!"

"Hey, somebody's been in here again," Corky added. "We sure didn't leave that mess."

The table was full of food and dirty dishes. It was as though someone had been interrupted right in the middle of a meal and left in an enormous hurry when he heard them coming.

"Looks as though someone was pretty hungry," Dad said, inspecting the remains on the table.

There was half a glass of milk, a handful of peanut-butter cookies from Mrs. Whipple's cooky jar, a slab of Swiss cheese, some butter and crackers, and a jar of pickles.

No wonder the liver had disappeared, Mik thought. The prowler had probably taken that too.

Bowser investigated the crumbs spilled on the floor.

"After him!" Mik coaxed. "Go get him!"

Bowser, however, simply wagged his tail and looked friendly. He wasn't exactly a watchdog.

It was Bud who first saw the hat. "Hey," he said. "Look at that."

It was a brown felt hat with a red feather stuck in its band.

"Mr. Mo's hat," Pete said happily.

And it was. It surely was Mr. Monroney's hat.

"But it couldn't have been Mr. Monroney," Mom said quickly. "He wouldn't break into Mrs. Whipple's house."

Not one of them wanted to believe it was Mr. Monroney, and yet there was his hat, and Mik *had* mentioned to him that Mrs. Whipple would be away. He did know she had gone to Monterey.

Mik had to say something. "The prowler probably stole Mr. Monroney's hat," he suggested.

Everyone agreed immediately. "That's probably exactly what happened," Dad said. "I'm sure of it."

Dad and Bud went on an inspection tour of the house, with Mik and Corky following close behind, Mom next, and Pete last, all tangled up with Bowser, Cassandra, and Fredericka.

Dad took a careful look at the window and discovered that it had been pried open with a crowbar. Bud looked in the drawers and closet and murmured knowingly, "Doesn't look as though anything's been touched."

Mother nodded. "I don't think the prowler did a thing but eat the food. The poor soul was probably hungry."

Now Mom was beginning to feel sorry for the prowler. She couldn't bear to see anything go hungry—not even a dog or a cat. The thought of somebody actually being hungry enough to break into a house almost made her weep. "Imagine having to steal in order to eat," she said thoughtfully.

Mik tried to think whether Mr. Monroney had looked especially hungry lately. He wasn't fat, but he surely wasn't skinny either. His cheeks were pink, and his stomach seemed a good comfortable size—not big, but not flat. And if he were really hungry, he could always eat his ice cream. Mik tried to get Mr. Monroney out of his mind, but the fact remained that his hat was indeed there, sitting right in the middle of Mrs. Whipple's kitchen.

Dad was sure nothing more had been disturbed, but he decided to call Officer Mitchell anyway. Officer Mitchell was an old friend. He was the one who had found Mik roaming around town when he was five years old and brought him home after Mom had frantically searched every store on Shattuck Avenue.

"Children and dogs—they're my specialty," he had said, and he had helped them find Bowser too, when he was still a puppy and had run away.

While Dad talked to Officer Mitchell on the phone, Mik and Corky slipped back into the kitchen. Mik took Mr. Monroney's hat and looked for a place to hide it. He didn't want to give Officer Mitchell any unnecessary ideas, even though he was a good fellow.

"How about the garbage can?" Corky suggested.

But Mik couldn't put Mr. Monroney's precious good-luck

hat in a garbage can—even an empty one. He looked all around, finally opened the oven, and stuffed in the hat just as Dad came in.

When Officer Mitchell arrived, no one mentioned the hat. He looked around quickly, checking closets, drawers, and windows.

"Not much harm done from what I can see," he said. "I'll come by from time to time to keep an eye on things," he added reassuringly. "There isn't much more we can do. Why don't you folks go on home and stop worrying?"

"I don't think I'll write Mrs. Whipple, then," Mom said. "I'd hate to spoil her vacation."

Officer Mitchell shook his head. "No need for that at all," he said. "I'll come by as often as I can, and we can alert the neighbors too."

He had no sooner mentioned the neighbors when there was a banging at the door. It was Mr. Potts again, red face, cane, and all.

"I saw your car out front," he said, turning to Dad, "and I want you to know your boy is responsible for the loss of my birds. The ring-necked pheasant can never be replaced, and I shall see that the cats are punished."

Dad listened quietly, waiting for him to finish. Then he said very calmly, "How do you know the cats actually ate your birds, Mr. Potts? Did you see them?"

Mr. Potts chose to ignore Dad's question. "They've had an eye on my birds for months," he went on. "Who else would break into my aviary?"

Dad had told Officer Mitchell about Mr. Pott's birds too, and now he turned to Mr. Potts and spoke up. "There's been a prowler in Mrs. Whipple's house today," he said. "He might very well have done some snooping in your yard too, you know."

"Sure," Bud agreed. "I'll bet that's who stole your birds, Mr. Potts."

Of course, Mik thought, that must be the answer. But what about Mr. Monroney's hat? If it was Mr. Monroney, he surely wouldn't steal the birds, would he?

When Mr. Potts heard about the prowler, he decided he'd better hurry home. He had left his rear door un-latched, and things certainly didn't sound very safe. He stamped out of the house, muttering about his rights and lawyers and suits and the pound.

"Really," Mother said, "what an impossible old man. He must be terribly unhappy to act like that."

"Oh, he's unhappy, all right," Officer Mitchell ex-plained. "He's never been the same since his wife died."

But Mik didn't feel a bit sorry for him. "He's the mean-est ogre I've ever seen," he muttered. Even Bowser, who never growled at anybody except the garbage man, growled and bared his teeth at Mr. Potts.

"Don't worry, Mik," Dad said. "We'll have another talk with Mr. Potts someday when he's not so upset."

And then, when no one else could hear, he added, "Don't

forget the hat, Mik. I doubt if baked felt would taste too good."

Dad had known all along, and he hadn't said a word to anyone.

CHAPTER 5

The Job for Dad

Mr. Monroney's good-luck hat sat on the hall table of the Watanabe house for two whole days. For two days no one had heard the bells of Mr. Monroney's ice-cream cart, and Mik began to wonder if maybe he was the mysterious prowler after all. He wondered what Mr. Monroney would say when he handed him the hat and told him where he had found it.

At last, on the third day, just as Mik and Corky were trying to teach Carmichael how to whistle reveille, Mik heard the bells. Carmichael hadn't so much as opened his beak, much less tried to whistle. He simply cocked his green head, blinked, and stared moodily at Mik and Corky as though he wanted them to go away. All he wanted to do, it seemed, was sit peacefully in the sun and eat a sunflower seed or two.

Mik grabbed Mr. Monroney's hat and ran out into the street.

"Look, Mr. Monroney!" he shouted, waving the hat at him. "Look what we found!"

"We found it at Mrs. Whipple's," Corky added. "In her kitchen."

Mr. Monroney looked pale, and he wore a bright red kerchief around his throat. "I've got laryngitis," he whispered hoarsely. "First I lose my good-luck hat, and now I lose my voice. I may lose my mind next," he grumbled.

He was clearly delighted, however, to see his hat again. "Where did you say you found it?" he asked. He brushed it off and laid it lovingly on top of his cart. "I thought I was going to lose all my luck," he explained.

Quickly, in great bunches of words, Mik and Corky told Mr. Monroney about the prowler and about the food on the table and about Mr. Potts and his birds.

Mr. Monroney listened carefully and then asked again, "You say you found the hat in Mrs. Whipple's kitchen?"

Mik and Corky nodded. "That's where it was," Mik said again.

"Hmmmm," Mr. Monroney said. "That's very curious, very curious indeed. There is someone who has admired my hat for some time. I wonder if maybe while I was having coffee at Walt's Diner. . . . Hmmmmm. I did leave it on the cart outside. Maybe . . ."

Clearly, Mr. Monroney hadn't been the prowler at all, but he certainly seemed to know who the prowler might have been.

"Who was it?" Mik asked anxiously. "Who d'you think?"

"Do you think he stole Mr. Potts's birds, too?" Corky asked.

Mr. Monroney tugged at his mustache, but he didn't say anything more. Quite suddenly he said he had some business to attend to, and he pushed his cart on up the street.

There was something very strange about Mr. Monroney and his hat and the prowler. He surely knew more about it all than he was telling.

That night at supper, as Mik made a crater for the gravy in his mashed potatoes, Dad said something once more about needing an assistant.

"The lawns are growing like weeds and begging for water in all this heat," he said. "Want to earn a little extra money for that new Shakespeare reel you want, Bud?" he asked.

Bud swallowed and looked troubled. "Gosh, Dad," he said, "you should've asked me yesterday. I just promised Mr. Lane I'd help him deliver for his drugstore this summer. In fact, I start next week."

Dad ran a hand over the short bristles of his hair. "I didn't realize you were in such demand, Bud," he said. "Well, I guess I'll make out."

"Can't you hire one of the college boys for the summer?" Mom asked. But Dad thought they had all gone home long ago, or gotten jobs if they were staying in Berkeley.

Mik carefully ate the potato around his lake of brown gravy. He wanted to ask Dad if he could be his assistant, but he knew Dad would just say no. He'd already proved he wasn't reliable as an assistant. Mik thought of what he could do with some extra money. He could buy some birds for Mr. Potts and make him promise not to harm Cassie and Freddie. He could even buy a present for Mrs. Whipple to make up for having let a prowler in her house. Mik broke the edge of the crater now and let the gravy spill over his plate like a great brown flood.

"I help you," Pete said to Dad.

Mik scarcely heard when Dad spoke to him.

"Would you, Mik?" he asked.

"Huh? Would I what?"

"Like a job with me after you've finished at Mrs. Whipple's?" Dad asked.

Mik felt himself grinning from one ear to the other. "Who, me?" he asked. "You mean me?"

Dad reached over and poked him in the ribs. "You!" he said. "In fact, you can come along for half a day tomorrow if you like—just to try things out."

Mik looked at Mom, expecting her to tell him he'd better concentrate on one job at a time, but life was full of surprises tonight. "It would be nice for you, Mik," she said. "Why don't you forget about Mr. Potts for a while and go have a good time with Dad?"

"I watch Bowser and Carm for you," Pete offered.

"Just don't leave the hose turned on at anybody's house," Bud warned, but Mik didn't need to be reminded. He'd do everything right this time. He was determined to do one job right this summer.

The next morning Mik set out with his father at seven

o'clock. The morning was fresh and cool, and the lawns were tipped with beads of dew. The sun was just breaking through the morning fog as Mik and his father drove up toward the seminary at the top of the hill.

"Today's my heavy day," Dad explained. "I've got six gardens to do, and the seminary garden isn't exactly small."

Mik nodded. He wondered if Dad might let him use the power mower on the big lawn. He helped unload the equipment, and then he waited. Dad looked at the mower and then at the sprayer, and then at Mik.

"I've got to spray the roses," he said. "Think you could handle the mower?"

"Could I!" Mik had watched Bud use it so many times, he was sure he could do it blindfolded. He'd not only mow the lawn, he would trim the edge and sweep the walk before Dad even finished his spraying. He'd show Dad what a good job he could do. He pushed the mower toward the lawn without waiting to hear anything more.

"Take it easy, Mik," Dad cautioned. "We still have other gardens to do after this one."

But Mik hadn't heard. Already he'd turned on the mower and with an enormous *vvvvrooooom*, he began to clip the lawn. Mik was sure it must be at least half as big as a football field. He began at the edge and decided to go around and around until he came to the middle. He wondered if he could end up right smack in the center of the grass. He went as fast as the mower would go—around and around and around. He didn't look to the right or to the left. He didn't look up to see where the sun rested in the sky. He kept his eyes on the mower and the blades of grass that whirled into the catch. When the catch was full, he emptied it in a large square of burlap, just as he'd seen his father do.

Suddenly Mik stopped. He knew someone was standing behind him, even though he couldn't see. It was like having a pair of feelers at the back of his head. Mik wheeled around, and there was Dad, standing with his hands on his hips.

"You having a race with somebody, Mik?" he asked.

Mik grinned and wiped his face. He suddenly realized how warm he was. He felt as though he had been working for two hours, but when he heard the bells of the campanile on the campus below, they were striking eight o'clock. Classes were just beginning.

"Come here a minute, Mik," Dad said. "Turn off the mower and come on over."

Mik followed his dad down the walk beside the chapel, toward the rose bed he had been spraying.

Dad pointed as they walked along. "Ever see a Peace rose climb up a trellis like that?" he asked. "Did you know they grew so tall?" Mik shook his head.

"And look here, Mik. The pink calla lilies I put in last year are beginning to bloom." Dad stepped over to a big green bush and pulled one of its branches toward Mik. "Smell this pittosporum, Mik. Some people call it mock orange. Smells just like the orange blossoms your mother carried at our wedding."

Dad smiled as he remembered, and then continued along the walk, pointing to this plant and to that. He would tell Mik the name of one and then crush the leaves of another for Mik to smell. Suddenly he pointed to a quick movement in the bush. "There's a linnet, Mik. See it with the red breast and the dark stripes on its belly? Watch it go after that worm."

Mik nodded and did as he was told, but he thought they were wasting an awful lot of time. There was so much to do before noon when he had to go home. He was anxious to get back to work.

"Uh-huh," he said impatiently, as Dad told him how he had mulched the camellias and would be setting in dahlia bulbs soon.

Finally Dad sat on one of the stone benches and motioned for Mik to sit beside him.

"There's a lot more to gardening than just seeing how fast you can get your work done, Mik," he began. "You must learn to know the living things you're working with, and if you understand them and love them, they'll grow to be beautiful for you. Look around, Mik. And I mean really look. Smell that grass you've just cut. Doesn't it make you glad to be alive and outdoors? And if your back aches, stop to stretch and feel the sun on your face. The outdoors is full of wonderful growing things, Mik, and if you keep your eyes open, you'll never stop learning, and you'll be able to make gardens you can be proud of. Know what I mean, Mik?"

That was about as long a speech as Mik had ever heard his dad give. Mik nodded.

"O.K., Pop," he said, but already he was aching to get back to the lawn. He did notice a spotted towhee, though, and as he saw it scurry across the lawn, he wished it were a ring-necked pheasant he could catch for Mr. Potts.

Mik saw Dad go back to pruning the canes from the yellow rose that climbed the chapel wall. He knew Dad liked being outside and working with plants and flowers better than anything else. In fact, he always said he wished he could do away altogether with things like sidewalks and ten-story buildings and super freeways. If he'd had his way, he would have been growing melons and lettuce in the San Joaquin Valley. He would be working with the soil and living on top of a knoll surrounded by oak trees, and maybe he would have a cow or two. It was a dream Dad liked to talk about now and then, just as Mik liked to take out his telescope every now and then to look at the stars.

But Mom was different. She loved the city. She had grown up in San Francisco and wouldn't hear of living on a farm. At least, that was the way Dad told the story. He said Mom wanted to be near shops and people and conveniences. So they had come to Berkeley where Mom could have her conveniences and San Francisco just across the bay, and Dad could still work outdoors and be close to growing things.

"It hasn't been a bad arrangement at all," Dad said. "Not bad at all." And Mik knew he meant it, because Dad was one of the happiest people he knew.

Mik remembered to take a deep breath as he went back to his lawn. He thought how much fun Bowser would have, running around up here, and then he thought of Carmichael, and then of Mr. Potts's birds, and soon the whole dismal cloud of worry came right back to hover around his head.

Mik knew he simply had to do something about Mr. Potts's birds before Mrs. Whipple came back. If Dad would give him a slight advance in salary, Mik thought, maybe he could buy Mr. Potts some parakeets and make him promise to leave Cass and Freddie alone.

The more Mik thought about it, the sooner he wanted to get over to Mr. Potts to make his proposition. Before Mik knew it, he was racing around the big lawn once more, and it wasn't until he had finished mowing the whole stretch of grass that he remembered to stop and look up at the sky. It was blue and clear, and the sun felt good on his face.

CHAPTER 6

Mik's Idea

The fog rolled in early that afternoon, and even before Mik finished watering Mrs. Whipple's garden, great gray drifts swept in from the ocean like a thick, furry flood. Mik shivered as he turned off the hose. Cassie and Freddie had been out for a half hour now, and Corky was inside, getting their supper ready for them.

Mik had just wound up the hose and was ready to go in when he saw Mr. Potts. He was standing in his yard beside his aviary, looking at the lone dove left inside. He was speaking to it in a voice so gentle that Mik could scarcely believe it was Mr. Potts.

Mik decided this was the time to tell him of his plan to buy some parakeets for him, even though he was positive—well, almost positive—that Cassie and Freddie had not eaten his birds.

"Mr. Potts," he began.

But besides being lame and cranky, Mr. Potts was also hard of hearing. He didn't so much as turn his head.

"Mr. Potts," Mik shouted, and this time Mr. Potts turned around.

"Eh? What? Who called?" he asked. When he saw Mik, the usual scowl returned to his face, and Mik almost wished he hadn't called. Somehow, he couldn't find any words.

"I . . . uh . . . I'm going to buy you some parakeets so you won't do anything to Cassie and Freddie," he stammered.

Mr. Potts didn't even look pleased. He simply continued to scowl and said, "Now what makes you think any birds you could buy would ever take the place of Gladys and Henry? Do you know what it means to lose a pet you've taken years to train? Why, Gladys and Henry used to sit on my shoulder and rub their beaks on my ear. They'd eat from my hand and fly back into the aviary when I told them to. You could never replace them. And as for my pheasant, well, that's something you'll never find in a pet shop, young man!"

Mik didn't know what to say. He had thought he would please Mr. Potts by offering to buy him some birds, and all he did was turn purple and red and get mad all over again.

As Mik stood there, digging his hands into his pockets, Cassie and Freddie scampered back toward the house, their bells jingling as they ran.

"Too late for bells now," Mr. Potts said darkly. "They

won't need those at the pound." And he stomped back to his house like a bear stalking to its cave.

It hadn't done a bit of good to talk to Mr. Potts. Mik knew now that he had to do more than buy parakeets at the pet shop to keep Mr. Potts from harming Cassie and Freddie. But what could he do? How would he ever, ever replace the birds that Mr. Potts had trained?

As Mik threw the flowered cover over Carmichael's cage that night, he had the beginning of an idea.

"Good night, old boy," Mik said.

Carmichael blinked and shrieked, "Hello, boy! *Sayonara!*" He could always make Mik smile, even when he felt miserable and blue.

"Carmichael's a pretty nice fellow, isn't he?" Mom said.

Of all the people in the Watanabe household, Mom and Mik were the two who liked pets best. Oh, everybody else liked them too, all right, but they didn't pick them up off the streets as Mom and Mik did. Right now, Mik had only Bowser and Carmichael, but there had been a time when he had a pet garter snake named Smiley; a turtle, Alexander the Great; a toad, Squeegee; and two fleas, Samson and Delilah. He had intended to train the fleas for a flea circus, but they disappeared from their matchbox house and probably went home to Bowser.

All Mom had now was a tank of tropical fish, but before that she had taken in a stray cat, which they called Scrooge because he looked so miserly and grumpy. One day last month, however, Scrooge had disappeared as mysteriously as he had come, and that was the end of him.

As Mik put Carmichael to bed now, he remembered what Mr. Potts had said about losing a trained pet. He wondered how he would feel if he thought somebody's cats had eaten Carmichael. He knew he would feel pretty terrible, but he'd still have Bowser and Mom's fish and everybody else in the family. Mr. Potts didn't have anybody except the mourning dove that seemed always to tell the world how sad life was. What Mr. Potts wanted were birds he could talk to. One who would talk back, of course, would be even better.

That night after he'd gone to bed, the idea began to take shape—slowly, slowly—in Mik's mind. It wasn't at all like Mom's quick ideas that suddenly came to her as she scrubbed behind Pete's ears or while she ironed Dad's shirts. Mik's ideas always came gradually, like the prize that comes in a surprise ball after you unwind yards and yards of crepe-paper strips. He could never make up his mind in a flash, the way Petey could, for instance. If you asked Pete whether he wanted a piece of cake or a dish of ice cream, he could tell you in a second. So could Bud. Mik always had to ponder a while over most things, but once he decided, he didn't change his mind.

Mik didn't tell anybody about his idea—not even Dad or Mom or Bud. He simply curled up tight around it, like a hand closing over a pebble, and thought about it until he fell asleep. He did decide, however, that he would discuss it with Mr. Monroney the next afternoon. That he would do for sure.

The next afternoon, when Mik heard the bells of Mr. Monroney's cart, he ran halfway down the street to meet him. Then he quickly told him of his idea. "Shall I do it?" he asked. "Shall I?"

Mr. Monroney rubbed his chin, pulled at his mustache, and then picked up his hat and put it on his head. "Helps me think more clearly," he explained briefly.

He was silent for a long time—at least it seemed a long time to Mik. Then, finally, he said, "I think it's a very fine idea, Mik. I do indeed. It might be just the thing that old duffer needs—a friendly gesture from someone like you."

Mr. Monroney was quiet again, and then he murmured, "I wish I could find out . . ." and then he stopped. "Go ahead, Mik, if you really want to do it."

"You think it's a good idea?"

"Sure, Mik. Sure."

"You don't care?"

"Of course not. Carmichael belongs to you now."

So Mik ran inside. "I'm going to give Carmichael to Mr. Potts," he said, "and make him promise to leave Cass and Freddie alone."

Mom was washing some dishes at the sink, but she stopped right in the middle of scouring a pan. "Why, Mik," she said, "that's very generous of you. I'm sure he'll agree not to harm Cassie and Freddie after that."

Mik was sure, too. After all, Carmichael was better than two trained parakeets. He could talk. And if Mr. Potts had Carmichael to talk to, he would surely feel more friendly toward Mrs. Whipple and her cats.

Mik put Carmichael and his cage in the basket of his bike and rode slowly to Mr. Potts's. He took Bowser along so he wouldn't feel too lonely coming back. As he got closer to Mr. Potts's house, however, he wondered more and more whether this was such a good idea after all. He went around and around the block five times, before he finally decided to go ahead.

Mik planned his words carefully because he knew he had to say just exactly the right thing in the right way. He took a deep breath and rang the bell.

Mr. Potts came to the door and peered at Mik through the upper half of his bifocals. "Oh, it's you," he said in a most unfriendly manner.

Mik thrust Carmichael at Mr. Potts and blurted out, "I'm giving you my pet parrot so you won't be lonesome, because he talks, and you've got to promise not to do anything to Cassie or Freddie or Mrs. Whipple."

Mik got it all out in one breath and waited for Mr. Potts to say something. But Mr. Potts looked as though he had swallowed his false teeth. He moved his mouth soundlessly for a minute and then sputtered, "Your pet parrot, eh? And you say he talks?" He peered at Carmichael and reached for the cage.

"In three languages," Mik explained. "He's very tal-

ented." Then, quickly, he added, "And you have to promise —about Cassie and Freddie."

Mr. Potts continued to inspect Carmichael without answering Mik. Then, suddenly, Carmichael burst out with "Hello, boy! *Sayonara! Dasvedanya!*" and he even tried to whistle two short scraggly little hoots.

"Atta boy, Carmichael!" Mik said proudly. "See, English, Japanese, and Russian. He's talented."

For a minute Mik thought Mr. Potts was going to break down and smile. There was a faint flicker at the corners of his mouth. Then, just as quickly, it was gone. He screwed up his face into its usual scowl and said, "So he really talks, does he?" Then without even thanking Mik, he closed the door and disappeared, taking Carmichael with him.

"*Sayonara!*" Carmichael squawked sadly.

"You didn't promise!" Mik shouted to Mr. Potts. But he was gone.

"He didn't promise," Mik said miserably to Bowser. "He didn't even promise."

Bowser wagged his tail and licked Mik's hand, but Mik didn't feel comforted at all. Carmichael was gone, and all for nothing. He was right back where he had started. Mik could have kicked himself for having had such a stupid idea.

Mik couldn't go home and tell everybody what had happened. He decided he would go look at Mrs. Whipple's lawn. It didn't need watering, however, and it was too early to feed the cats. There was nothing to do but go on home.

"C'mon, boy," Mik said to Bowser, but Bowser was making queer sounds deep down in his throat.

Mik looked up and thought he saw something move behind the curtain at the kitchen window. Had the prowler come back? Had he broken in because he knew Mik wouldn't be there until later? Mik wanted to burst into the house and catch the prowler red-handed. But suppose he was six feet tall? And suppose he had a gun?

Mik looked down at Bowser. "Want to go get the prowler, old boy?" he asked.

Bowser wagged his tail and looked friendly.

Mik thought of running home for help, but by the time he got back, the prowler would surely be gone. If he was going to catch him, he had to go in right now. Mik decided it wouldn't hurt to give the prowler a little warning. He jiggled the key in the lock and pushed the door open with a soft squeak.

"Come out, whoever you are!" Mik shouted. "Come on out!"

He stood back and waited. He listened, but all he could hear was the *drip-drip* of water at the sink. He held his breath and felt a prickling at the back of his neck. He pushed Bowser in ahead of him and walked cautiously into the kitchen. There was nothing on the table today except an empty glass. Had he and Corky left it there yesterday? Or had the prowler been back, after all?

Suddenly Mik heard a scuffling behind him and he

whirled, ready to throw the glass at the prowler. But it turned out to be only Cassie and Freddie. "Meowrrr," they said, sounding perfectly happy and serene.

"Who was in here?" Mik asked, but all they did was rub against Mik's legs and purr gently.

Mik went to the bedroom next and saw that the window was closed, but the latch was unfastened just as it had been before. There *had* been someone in the house after all. He had come in and then hurried out when Mik arrived. It was pretty spooky, all right, and Mik locked the window in a hurry and decided to get out.

"Whoever you are, you'd better stay out!" Mik shouted into the empty house, and then he slammed the door, turned the key in the lock, and called to Bowser.

"C'mon, boy, we're leaving," he said, and he ran home as fast as he could go.

CHAPTER 7

A New Complication

The prowler was still prowling, Carmichael was gone, and Mrs. Whipple was about to come home. Mik had done just about the worst job possible. Not a single thing had gone right.

"But you tried," Mother said consolingly. "You truly tried, and you did the best you could, Mik. That's what matters."

"I'm sure Mrs. Whipple can have a talk with Mr. Potts and straighten everything out," Dad added.

But Mik didn't want that. He had wanted to get everything straightened out before she came back. After all, she had trusted him with Cassie and Freddie. Now, she would come home on Saturday to find that he had made one glorious mess of everything.

At home, too, things didn't seem right without Carmichael.

"It does seem quiet," Mom said, although she was often the one who wanted to cover him up for the night because he made so much noise. "I do believe I miss him," she said.

Petey missed him too. Carmichael was always such a good target. Pete would aim his water pistol at him, say, "Bang, I got you. You're in jail," and there good old Carmichael would sit, behind his bars. He would cock his green head, stare at Petey, and say, "Hello, boy," no matter how many times he was squirted.

Even Bowser seemed to miss Carmichael. He sniffed around the house as though he had misplaced an old bone and went out at night to howl at the moon.

Mik knew that giving Carmichael to Mr. Potts had been the same kind of mistake he'd made when he offered to help with the dishes every night. They both seemed like fine ideas at the time, but caused nothing but misery afterward.

"I never should have done it," Mik said sorrowfully.

But Dad didn't think so. "You know, Mik," he said, "something good may come of it after all. You never can tell."

Life was a problem, all right. Mik sat on the porch with Bowser and told him all about it, and good old Bowser made sympathetic noises and licked Mik's hand. He could be a great comfort, Bowser could.

Mrs. Whipple had written Mik that she would be home about noon on Saturday. By ten o'clock Mik and Corky were sitting on her front steps.

"What time is it?" Mik asked Corky for about the tenth time.

"Almost eleven," Corky answered. "Another hour to go."

Mik sighed and wished Mrs. Whipple would hurry. He wanted to tell her everything and get it over with.

He looked up the street, hoping he would see Mrs. Whipple, but instead he saw Clancy Berryman, the monster ogre. Clancy strolled past Mrs. Whipple's house and looked at Mik and Corky.

"She's coming home today?" he asked.

Mik nodded.

"Too bad," Clancy muttered and went on down the street, kicking a pebble with his toe.

Mik wondered what he meant by that. Why was it too

bad? Did he know about all Mik's troubles? But even if he did, why should he care?

"What time is it?" he asked again.

"Five after eleven," Corky informed him.

Five minutes could drag like a sack of wet sand when you were waiting for somebody.

Then, finally, a yellow cab swerved around the corner, sped up to the house, and screeched to a stop. Mrs. Whipple came out breathless, clutching at the hat that sat askew on her head, like a cherry sliding off a mound of ice cream.

"My goodness," she murmured. "I wasn't *that* anxious to get home."

Then she saw Mik and Corky. "Why, what a lovely wel-come, Mikitaro and Cortland!" she said.

She bustled toward them, her arms full of bundles, and swept the two of them inside. In less than a minute Cassandra and Fredericka were in her arms, getting a good solid hugging.

"My, they look wonderful," she said, stroking their silky backs, "and the garden does too. You did a fine job, Mik."

Mik couldn't wait another minute. "But I didn't," he said dismally. "I didn't at all."

Then, in a tremendous shower of words that fell like rain in a summer storm, Mik and Corky told Mrs. Whipple everything. They didn't even give her a chance to take off her coat or hat. They told her about the open window and the hungry prowler. They told about Mr. Potts's birds and his threats to Cassie and Fred. When they'd finished, at last, Mrs. Whipple sat down.

"My gracious," she said. "Who in the world could have broken into my house?"

Mik looked at Corky, and Corky looked at Mik. Neither of them said a word about Mr. Monroney or about his good-luck hat. After all, it was clear that he wasn't the prowler, and he didn't seem ready to tell them anything more even if he knew who it was.

Mrs. Whipple sat on her couch, thinking. She was just like Mik's mother, however, when it came to hungry people. She simply couldn't get angry.

"Poor soul," she murmured gently. "Imagine anyone's being so hungry he would break into my house to find something to eat."

Then Mik told Mrs. Whipple about giving Carmichael to Mr. Potts, and for a minute he was afraid she was going to cry.

"Why, Mikitaro," she said, "that was a very sweet, unselfish thing for you to do, giving him your own pet."

And Mik had to back away quickly to escape something that looked like the beginning of a hug. He had to watch out for those around Mrs. Whipple. She always wanted to give them to people—especially if they had done something she considered noble or kind.

"Mr. Potts wouldn't promise, though," Mik explained quickly.

"He just took Carmichael and closed the door in Mik's face," Corky added. "He's a real ogre, all right."

Mrs. Whipple bristled. "Why, the idea!" she said. "I think he has behaved abominably, and I shall march right over and tell him so. The idea! Blaming you and threatening Cassie and Freddie, and taking Carmichael on top of that!"

At any rate, Mrs. Whipple wasn't angry at all with Mik even though he had been most unreliable. In fact, she didn't even seem very worried about the prowler.

"You did a good job, Mik," she said. "And you just stop worrying. I shall speak to Mr. Potts and straighten everything out."

When Mrs. Whipple had a chance to open her bags at last, she had presents for everybody. Thermometers set in abalone shells for Mik and Corky, a mounted butterfly from the Butterfly Trees for Bud, and a bag full of sea shells for Petey. She also had an envelope for Mik with the money he had earned.

"I don't think I should take it," Mik began. "I didn't do a very good job."

But Mrs. Whipple gave him a pat on the head. "Mikitaro Watanabe," she said, "you just take this and scoot along home, or I'll give you a good hugging."

Mik didn't wait to hear any more. Besides, he was anxious to give Corky his share. He thanked Mrs. Whipple and rushed away before she could even shake his hand.

When he got home, he discovered a completely new complication in his life. Dad had gotten a phone call from

Mr. Kato, whom everyone called the pillar of the Elm Street Japanese Church. Mik tried to picture him in the corner of the chapel, one hand on his hip, the other raised high, holding up one of the beams. "He is surely the pillar of the church," everyone said, and around the Watanabe household they got to calling him Mr. Kato, the pillar. That is, except for Petey, who always called him Mr. Pillow.

At any rate, Mr. Kato, the pillar, called Dad to say that he had some fine news. Mr. Mihara, who was coming from Japan to be the new minster of their church, had just sent a cable. He was arriving a month ahead of schedule so that he would have time to get settled before he began his studies at the seminary. He was going to go to school part time and preach at their church on Sundays. This was a good thing for the grandmas and grandpas, because Mr. Mihara could speak both English and Japanese, and he could give them their sermon in Japanese. Mr. Mihara's son Tamio was coming three weeks earlier than his parents, with a missionary friend who was paying his plane fare. Could the Watanabes take Tamio in for a couple of weeks until his family arrived, Mr. Kato wanted to know.

"Of course," Dad said immediately. "We'd be glad to."

When Mom heard the news, she got excited. It wasn't that she minded having Tamio coming to stay. She was used to having Mik or Bud bring home a friend. Whoever had the guest stayed in the bedroom, and the other one slept on the living-room couch. The part that excited her was that the Miharas would be coming a whole month earlier than she'd

family

expected. As president of the Women's Guild at church, she was in charge of getting the parsonage ready.

"We haven't even begun," she said anxiously. "The kitchen cupboards need painting, the bedrooms need curtains, the living room should be repapered, and the sink has a leak!"

As Mom got more and more flustered, Dad tried to calm her.

"Now, Helen, don't get excited," he cautioned. "You still have three weeks, and you know you don't have to fix up the parsonage all by yourself. Get the others to help."

Mom was always being appointed chairman of all kinds of committees, but she usually ended up doing most of the work by herself. "I hate to bother other people," she would say. "They're all so busy."

"You'll never make a good administrator, talking like that," Dad would say. "You've got to learn to let people help you."

But Mother said she didn't want to be an administrator at all. "I'm not trying to run a bank," she'd answer. And what could Dad say to that? She most certainly wasn't running a bank.

Most of the time Dad, Bud, and Mik would end up being her committee, and would have to do such chores as cleaning out the parsonage basement on a Saturday afternoon for instance.

Mom did stop worrying about painting and papering for

a few minutes now, just long enough to have one of her quick ideas.

"I just thought," she said, her face brightening. "We ought to start a camp fund for Tamio so we can send him to Camp Mohala with Mik. Maybe we could all sell soap for him at church. Wouldn't that be fun?"

It wasn't exactly Mik's idea of fun. Having a new boy tag along with him to camp was the last thing he needed. Mik pretended he hadn't heard.

Bud had his worries too. "I suppose I get to sleep on the couch," he said dismally. It was bad enough having two younger brothers, without having another little guy come to complicate matters and take his bunk on top of that.

"You won't mind, will you, Bud?" Mom asked.

"I guess not," Bud said reluctantly. Then he turned to Mik and gave him one of the biggest surprises of his life.

"Hey, want me to help you sell some of that Y soap?" he asked, as though he were simply offering Mik a piece of gum.

"Huh?" Mik asked. "What's the catch?"

He'd been trapped too often by Bud's "deals" to fall into such an easy trap. There was the time he had washed Mrs. Bigelow's huge German shepherd dog, for instance, because Bud had offered him fifty cents to do the job. He and Corky had gotten themselves soaked to the skin and then discovered afterward that Bud had been given seventy-five cents to do the job. He had earned twenty-five cents without doing a thing.

"Aw, don't be so suspicious," Bud protested. "I'm offering to help sell your soap so you can get to camp, that's all."

"For nothing?" Mik asked, still wary.

"Sure, for nothing. I'm a good guy—a real prince—that's all."

Mik trailed Bud upstairs to their room and watched as Bud sat on the lower bunk, folded his arms on his chest, and tried yoga.

"I'm a real prince on a golden charger," he said, closing his eyes. "You can take my offer or leave it."

Mik knew when to stop asking questions. "I take it," he said, and diving into the closet, he produced three boxes of soap.

"They're as good as sold right now," Bud said mysteriously. Then, slicking down his hair with some water, he went downstairs, whistling.

Something was pretty fishy, all right. But Mik didn't mind. After all the bad luck he'd had lately, he was ready for something good to come his way, even though it came from Bud and was slightly peculiar.

CHAPTER 8

Girls!

Bud and Mik usually didn't do very much talking after they got into their bunks—Bud on top and Mik below. Bud often read *Field and Stream* or *Scientific American,* and Mik read library books, mostly on outer space.

Tonight, however, things were different. For one thing, Tamio Mihara was arriving the next morning, and Dad and Mik were taking the morning off to go meet him. They would have to get up at six o'clock to be at the airport on time, and that was why Mom had shooed everyone off to bed especially early.

Bud wasn't going, of course, because he had his job at Lane's, but he'd come to bed anyway and lay in his bunk reading. Mik could tell by the way the pages of the magazine flipped, however, that Bud wasn't really reading.

"What d'you think Tamio will be like?" Mik asked.

The springs above his head squeaked. "I dunno," Bud answered briefly. "Hard to say."

Mik didn't feel a bit sleepy. He wanted to talk. "What's it like in back?" he asked. "I mean at Lane's."

"Oh, lots of bottles and jars full of powders and pills and stuff like that," Bud answered. He was quiet a while and then added something he knew would make Mik's eyes pop. "I get a free sandwich and malt for lunch every day. D'ja know that?"

"Wow! Any flavor you want?"

"Sure."

"Any kind of sandwich? Even salami?"

"Sure."

Mik whistled through his teeth. "Some job!" he said enviously. "Hey, Bud," he went on, now that Bud had begun to talk. "Who're you selling all that soap to, anyway?"

There was no answer from the upper bunk.

"Huh, Bud?"

"Somebody. Nobody you know." Bud had become about as talkative as a dead clam in a bucket of sand.

Mik could hear the busy ticking of the alarm clock beside his bed. It sounded as though it were rushing toward morning. Mik heard the springs squeak again as Bud flopped over in his bunk. Then, suddenly, he answered Mik's question.

"A friend of mine," he said. "She lives near Lane's."

"You mean a *girl's* buying your soap?" Mik asked. "A *girl?*"

"Sure," Bud answered, trying to sound very matter of fact. "Why not?"

"But a girl!" Mik went on.

"Well, they take baths. They wash," Bud said. "Besides, Jane sold those boxes to her mother and her aunt. Now her girl friend's selling some to *her* mother. I can sell more for you if you want."

Mik was flabbergasted. So that was how Bud was helping him sell his Y soap. He was selling it to a girl! That was why Bud cleaned his fingernails and slicked down his hair and wore white shirts. Bud liked girls! Well, if they helped buy his soap, Mik thought, he didn't mind—that is, for Bud. As for himself, he'd never have anything to do with girls, not in a million years.

Mik went to sleep feeling that he'd made quite a discovery.

Morning came so quickly, Mik didn't even hear the alarm. It unwound itself completely, and still Mik was sound asleep, his head stuffed under his pillow. He didn't wake up, in fact, until Dad came in and pulled off his covers.

"Come on, Mik," he coaxed. "We don't have much time. Mom and Petey have decided to come, too."

Mik scarcely knew what he was doing until they were all in the station wagon and driving over the bay bridge. He yawned and looked out over the sparkling bay and wondered what Tamio would be like. Mr. Kato had told them he would be arriving with a Mrs. Dinkelfeffer, who had taught in Japan for twenty-five years. "Just look for a gray-haired woman with a Japanese boy," he said. "I'm sure you won't be able to miss them."

Even at seven o'clock the airport was already crowded with people. A jet liner was about to take off, and Mik and Pete pressed their noses against the big windows of the terminal to watch as it taxied down the runway and then zoomed off. They watched until it grew smaller and smaller and finally became part of the sky. It gave Mik a lonely feeling to watch it disappear into nothing at all.

But soon Tamio's plane from Japan was announced over the loudspeaker. They all hurried down the ramp to the small waiting room and saw the plane taxi to a stop. The steps were pushed up and then people began to come out. Some were carrying bags and coats, some carried babies. Some wore leis of orchid and pea blossoms, and others carried them in little plastic bags.

Mik watched for a boy with a woman who might have a name like Dinkelfeffer, while Pete pointed to practically everyone who came off the plane.

"There they come," he would announce happily, but he was wrong every time. All the children seemed to belong to parents, and soon there were fewer and fewer people coming from the plane.

"I wonder where they could be," Mom said, sounding worried. "This is the right plane, isn't it?"

"Of course it is," Dad reassured her. "There are still a few more coming."

And then Mik saw the gray-haired woman carrying all

sorts of bundles tied up in a silk square. Someone walked along beside her, but it wasn't a boy at all. It was a Japanese girl with straight black hair. She looked just like one of Mom's Japanese dolls, but she was wearing Western clothes. What in the world had happened to Tamio? Mik wondered if they had met the wrong plane on the wrong day. Surely someone had made a mistake somewhere.

Mother and Dad waited anxiously, and Mik and Petey knelt on the red leather couch and pressed their noses against the window as they watched.

The gray-haired woman smiled and continued to walk straight toward them. Something was very strange. She came right up to Dad and said, "You must be Mr. Watanabe. I was told you would meet us."

Dad nodded. "And you are Mrs. Dinkelfeffer?" he asked.

"Yes, yes, that's quite right, and this is Tamiko," she said, pushing the little girl toward Dad.

Dad opened his mouth, but there were no words, no words at all. He closed it again.

"Tamiko?" Mom said. "But we thought . . . that is, we were expecting a boy, Tamio."

The little girl shook her head. "My name is Tamiko," she said firmly. "I am nine and I am a girl."

Mother laughed then and put an arm around her. "Why, of course you're a girl," she said. "And you don't know how delighted I am. I have a family of three boys! Did you come instead of your brother?"

Tamiko shook her head. "I have no brother," she said.

It took a good ten minutes for Mrs. Dinkelfeffer and Tamiko to explain that there had been a mistake somewhere. There was no Tamio at all. Tamiko had always been a girl, she said, and was the daughter of the Reverend and Mrs. Mihara of Setagaya District, Tokyo, Japan.

Dad shook his head. "How on earth did we get the idea you'd be a boy?" he asked.

It was Mom who answered. "Why, it must have been Mr. Kato," she said.

"Mr. Pillow," Petey added.

"Mr. Kato is the one who told us the Miharas had a boy Mik's age," she explained to Mrs. Dinkelfeffer. "That's why we were so confused."

What a mistake for anybody to make, Mik thought dismally, especially the pillar of the church! Now they'd be stuck with a girl in the house for three whole weeks. That was impossible. Mom would just have to get rid of her somehow.

Dad finally recovered and introduced Mik and Pete to Tamiko and Mrs. Dinkelfeffer. Mik looked at his shoes, and Pete slid down behind the arm of the couch.

"Ah, isn't he cunning," Mrs. Dinkelfeffer said.

Then, suddenly, she was surrounded by three breathless women wearing hats and gloves. They were from the Board of Foreign Missions and had come to meet Mrs. Dinkelfeffer. They would have been there on time, they said, if only they had been able to find a parking place closer by. Everyone agreed that parking was a terrible problem. Then the women shook hands with everybody, even with Mik. Pete, however, absolutely refused. The more they tried to make him, the further down he scrunched behind the arm of the couch with his eyes shut tight. He was like an ostrich. He thought that if he couldn't see them, they couldn't see him either. Mom was embarrassed.

"I think we'd better start for home," she suggested.

Mrs. Dinkelfeffer gave Tamiko an enormous hug. She looked like another big hug-giver. "I know you'll be in good hands, my dear," she said.

"Good-by," Tamiko said solemnly, and she bowed just as Grandma Watanabe always did.

As they walked to the baggage counter, Mik whispered to his mother. "When can we get rid of her?" But Mother didn't even answer. She put a quick finger to her lips and then turned to ask Tamiko if she had enjoyed her first plane ride.

"It was very much great fun," she answered carefully, "and the ocean was very enormously big." She spoke English anyway, Mik observed.

Tamiko sat up in front with Mom and Dad, and Pete got in back with Mik. Mik had to do something. He just couldn't sit there and watch the back of Tamiko's head, so he poked and tickled poor Pete until he gave up and cried "uncle." Then he stretched out on the floor and fell asleep. He was just like Bowser that way. He could curl up almost anywhere and fall asleep in less than a minute. It was a pretty convenient thing to be able to do.

As soon as they got home, Mik ran over to report the bad news to Corky.

"Honest," he said, when Corky refused to believe him. "Tamio turned out to be a girl. There's a girl living in our house!" That was about as bad a piece of luck, Mik thought, as losing Carmichael to Mr. Potts.

"Boy, that's tough," Corky agreed. "In fact, that's awful!" He had a little sister. He knew. He sat down on the curb with Mik and waited for Mr. Monroney.

When he came at last, he was wearing his hat on his head, and that surely meant a catastrophe. He must have known something terrible was going to happen, Mik thought, and it surely had.

"We have a girl at our house," Mik shouted before Mr. Monroney even reached them.

Instead of looking alarmed, however, Mr. Monroney smiled and took off his hat.

"Well, now," he said. "Well, well, I didn't know."

And he opened his cart and pulled out three orange popsicles. "It's on the house," he said, grinning. "We'll celebrate the arrival of a little sister for Mik."

Mik had already pulled the paper off his popsicle when he understood what Mr. Monroney thought.

"Gosh, Mr. Monroney, she's not ours," he explained quickly. "She's from Japan. We just have to keep her till her family comes." He held out his popsicle. "You want this back?" he asked.

Mr. Monroney laughed. "Ah, so it is that kind of girl. Well, never mind. Keep the popsicle. We can celebrate the coming of a girl from Japan."

"Me too?" Corky asked. "Shall I keep mine, too?"

"Sure, sure." Mr. Monroney nodded, and the three of them sat on the curb licking and sucking.

If felt good, Mik thought, to get his tongue around the sweet cold taste of orange, even if this wasn't a matter for celebration at all.

"Any more news about the prowler?" Mr. Monroney asked suddenly. "Hasn't anyone turned up to confess about stealing the birds?"

Mik shook his head. "Heck, no. Even Officer Mitchell says we'll probably never find out who it was."

"And Mik's lost Carmichael forever," Corky added glumly.

But Mr. Monroney didn't seem to think so at all. "Oh, I don't know," he said. "Maybe someday Mr. Potts will be moved to return Carmichael to Mik. Who knows?"

Mik knew, however, that there wasn't much chance of that—not with Mr. Potts. Why, he hadn't even promised to leave the cats alone when Mrs. Whipple herself went over to see him. All he had said was that he was thinking things over. No, there wasn't a chance of ever getting Carmichael back. Mik knew that for sure.

Suddenly, as he sat there licking his ice-cold popsicle, a wonderful idea occurred to him. If Tamiko was a girl, she wouldn't be going to Camp Mohala with him. Furthermore, she couldn't use the camp fund they were raising by selling Y soap at church. Maybe, if no one else needed it, they might even give it to Mik.

That was one good thing about Tamiko's being a girl. He punched Corky in the arm. "Hey," he said, grinning. "I won't have to take her to Camp Mohala!"

CHAPTER 9

A Discovery at the Park

Tamiko turned out to be quite a girl. Mik had never run across one like her before. There was the day, for instance, when he came home after helping Dad and found her rolling all over the living-room floor with Petey.

"There," she said, pinning him down. "Give up? Give up?"

Pete was shrieking with laughter. "Give up!" he shouted.

Mik felt he should say something on Pete's behalf.

"Heck, he's only four," he said. "He's a lot smaller than you."

"Okay," Tamiko said cheerfully. She helped Pete to his feet and then faced Mik. "I'll wrestle with you next."

Mik backed away just in time. "Heck, no," he said. "Not me. I'm not wrestling with any girl!"

He had to be careful around this one. She was pretty strange, all right. She not only wrestled, she liked to save boxes. She kept almost every box Mother threw away—

egg cartons, candy boxes, matchboxes, jello and cereal boxes
—everything. And she collected things—beads, thread, mar-
bles, leaves, flowers, rocks, insects, and butterflies. She sorted
them out and then put everything away in the boxes she had
saved. She liked butterflies best, and each time she went out
of the house, she carried an enormous white net that she
had brought from Japan. It was big enough, Mik was sure,
to catch a homing pigeon!

"It's very good for catching various specimens," Tamiko
declared, and whenever Mik went out, she would go along,
carrying this enormous net and waving it around like a
hunter on a safari. It was downright embarrassing for Mik.

"Why don't you leave that old sack home for a change?"
he would ask. But Tamiko didn't pay the slightest attention
to him. Dad wasn't much help either.

"I think it's a fine thing to be interested in nature," he
said. "You go right ahead, Tamiko, and make yourself a
good collection. I'll help you mount them if you like."

So naturally Tamiko collected more and more things and
waved her net around and kept right on embarrassing Mik.

"Never mind," she said as he sneered. "You watch. Some
day I will catch something truly wonderful in it."

"Uh-huh," Mik said. "Like a rhinoceros or something."

The thing that annoyed Mik the most, however, was that
she wanted to follow him everywhere. If he went to Corky's,
she wanted to go along. If he went to Mrs. Whipple's, she
went with him. She even came outside when he played with

Bowser, and Bowser, wagging his tail, would chase all the sticks she threw for him. He just didn't know any better.

"Why doesn't she trail Bud?" Mik would ask plaintively. "Or even Petey?"

But he got no sympathy from Mom. "After all, she's our guest," she would say. "We must see that she keeps well and happy until her parents come. It won't be long."

It was too long already as far as Mik was concerned.

"Girls can be a pain in the neck," Mik said to Dad as they rode to work together.

Dad grinned. "Buck up, old man," he said. "In a few more years it'll all be different."

Mik somehow managed to survive three weeks with a girl in the house, and then, finally, it was time for Mr. and Mrs. Mihara to come. They were to arrive on Saturday.

On Friday the ladies of the church gathered at the parsonage to give it a last-minute cleaning. Mom, the non-administrator, naturally tried to do most of the work. She brought along a mop to scrub the floor, she picked all the roses in the yard so the parsonage would smell like spring, and she also took along a pot of spaghetti for the ladies' lunch. She took Petey, and she took Tamiko to watch Pete.

Along about eleven o'clock when the ladies were just about finished with the cleaning, it began to rain. It wasn't a soft gentle sprinkle, but the hard driving rain that comes with a sudden storm. The sound of the rain in the gutters filled the gloomy rooms of the parsonage, and the ladies looked out the window and murmured that it was too bad to have rain just when the Miharas were about to arrive.

What Mik's mother said, however, was something more than that. "The roof is leaking!" she called from the upstairs bedroom. "It's leaking right on top of the bed!"

Petey immediately jumped on the bed. Then he opened his mouth, leaned back, and caught the next drop from the ceiling right in his mouth. It was quite an accomplishment.

But Mother was exasperated. "Oh, Petey," she said. "Close your mouth and run downstairs to the kitchen for a pan to catch the water."

"O.K.," Pete said.

He ran downstairs, carefully dodging two women who wanted to know if he was Mother's little helper, and headed straight for the table. It was higher than his head, of course, and he reached for the first pan he could see. Naturally, he didn't pick an empty one. He picked one full of spaghetti. Not only was it full of spaghetti, it was full of Mrs. Kato's spaghetti. She had brought some lunch for the ladies too. It came sloshing down all over Petey, covering him from head to foot with tomato sauce and meat balls.

"Wah!" Petey cried. "Wahhhhhh!"

Poor Mrs. Kato was the first to reach him. She saw what had happened to her lovely spaghetti, and for a minute she looked as though she had swallowed a hot marshmallow.

"Oh, my," she said, picking some strands of spaghetti off Petey's head and trying to find some kind words to say to him. But there Petey stood, covered with spaghetti and screaming like a fire engine headed for a five-alarm blaze.

Mrs. Watanabe and Tamiko rushed into the kitchen to see what had happened. And it was precisely at that moment that the cable arrived. It was from Tamiko's father, and it said that they would be delayed a few weeks. Tamiko's mother had caught a bad cold that had turned into pneumonia, and she couldn't travel until she was stronger.

"Oh," the ladies murmured, "what a shame!"

Now, however, they didn't have to worry about the leaky roof and the wet spot on the bed. They would have time to fix that before the Miharas arrived.

"You will stay with us, of course, until your parents arrive," Mrs. Watanabe said quickly to Tamiko. "In fact, you stay with us just as long as you like"

This was great news for Petey, and he stopped crying immediately. He liked having Tamiko to play with. For one thing, she was much more fun to shoot with his water pistol than Carmichael, because she would shoot back. "Bang!" she'd say. "I'm not so dead, after all. Bang!"

It wasn't such bad news for Tamiko either. She was disappointed, of course, not to have her mother and father coming. But on the other hand, she was having such a good time with the Watanabes, she didn't mind another few weeks there at all.

"I like being your daughter," she said to Mik's mother.

The only person who thought it was terrible news was Mik. He and Dad came home when it began to rain, and Mik decided this would be a fine time to paint his bicycle. He had just pried the lid off the can of blue paint when Mom, Petey, and Tamiko came home.

"They're not coming," Tamiko called down to him in the basement.

"Huh?" Mik asked vaguely.

"Come on up for a minute," Mom called.

Then she told both Mik and Dad about the cable.

"That's too bad," Dad said thoughtfully.

Mik couldn't help sounding disappointed. "You mean you're not leaving?" he asked Tamiko.

Mik's mother answered quickly for Tamiko. "No, she'll be staying until her parents come. Isn't that nice?"

This time it was Dad who answered quickly, before Mik could say no. "I'm sorry about your mother, Tamiko," he said, "but she will be well soon, and in the meantime we're glad to have you stay. You know, Mrs. Watanabe has always wanted a daughter."

"I have indeed," Mom said.

And then she had another of her flash ideas. "Why don't you take Tamiko to see the Junior Science Museum in the park, Mik?" she asked. She seemed to think that Tamiko needed cheering.

"O.K.," Petey said immediately.

Mik glared at him.

"Mik?" Mother asked, looking straight at him.

"Well, I was going to paint my bike," he began.

"Today?" she asked. "Now?"

"Uh-huh. I already opened the can of paint."

"It won't dry in this kind of weather," Dad said. "The Science Museum sounds better on a day like this."

Mik was outnumbered, surrounded, and as good as captured.

"It's raining," he said feebly.

"I'll drive you over," Mom offered.

This time, however, it was Tamiko who answered. "Oh,

no," she said. "We can walk. I can wear my new raincoat."

Mik groaned. Not only did he have to take Tamiko to the museum, he was going to have to walk there in the rain. He decided then and there that he would invite Corky to go along. If we was going to spend a whole damp afternoon with Tamiko in the Science Museum, he was going to take Corky along to suffer with him.

"O.K. Let's go, then," Mik said hopelessly. His day was ruined.

Tamiko put on her new raincoat and her new red rubber boots. Then, of all things, she went to the hall closet and got her big white butterfly net.

"Gollee, you're not taking that old thing today, are you?" Mik asked.

Tamiko nodded. "Sure," she said. "I might see something I want to catch."

"For Pete's sake," Mik said, thoroughly disgusted.

At which point Pete ran upstairs and got his cowboy holster. "Might see something to shoot," he said, flourishing his water pistol.

Mik sighed. It was a hard life, living in the same house with a girl and a little brother.

The rain had turned into a slow misty drizzle now, but the streets were still dismal and empty. Anybody with any sense would stay indoors, Mik thought miserably.

They stopped for Corky, and he said the same thing. "It's a crazy day to be going to the park," he said, but he was a loyal friend and he came along.

Tamiko marched along silently, her net resting on her shoulders like a gun. Petey marched behind her, ready to shoot the first moving thing that crossed his path.

The park was green and dripping. Drops of water still clung to the leaves of the trees, and the ground was soft and spongy. Mik knew now how to notice things, and he saw how everything looked clean and washed. The shrubs were wet-leafed, but the ground beneath them had safe, dry spots. A fat quail, its topknot quivering, scuttled quickly into the brush at the sound of their steps. Mik wondered if it had a nest somewhere nearby and peered into the bushes. That was when he saw the bird.

"Look!" he called.

There, beneath the bushes, crouched quietly in its shelter from the rain, was a pheasant—a beautiful ring-necked pheasant.

"I'll bet that's Mr. Potts's pheasant," Mik whispered hoarsely. "I'll bet that's just what it is."

Everybody stopped walking. Everybody stopped breathing. The bird was very still. It saw them, and yet it didn't seem frightened at all.

"That *is* Mr. Potts's pheasant," Corky whispered. "What'll we do?"

They *had* to catch it. They simply had to. Then they could prove once and for all that the cats hadn't eaten Mr. Potts's birds. It was the only way.

No one dared move for fear the bird would fly away. Even Petey knew enough to stay very still.

Then Tamiko turned to Mik and whispered softly. "I'll catch it for you," she said. "I'll catch it."

CHAPTER 10

A Bird for a Bird

Tamiko moved carefully, ever so carefully. She didn't make a sound as she glided closer and closer. She raised her net slowly, slowly in the air, took a quick step forward, and then *plop,* down it came right over the pheasant. There was a flurry of wings as the startled bird tried to escape, but Tamiko scooped it up in the net, and it was caught. It hadn't gotten away.

At last Mik dared to breathe once more. "You did it!" he said gleefully. "You caught it!" And he found himself slapping her on the back like an old buddy. The big white net had been useful for something after all. Like Mr. Monroney's good-luck hat, it could be a pretty handy thing to have around.

"Hey, that was pretty neat," Corky said with just a hint of admiration in his voice. "In fact, it was real neat."

Petey didn't try to hide his admiration at all. "You got

him, Tamiko," he said, jumping up and down. "You got him!"

Of course no one was thinking about the Science Museum now. And no one paid any attention whatever to the water dripping from the trees or the wet, squishy grass. They turned right around and headed straight for Mr. Potts's house. They decided first, however, to stop at Mrs. Whipple's.

Keeping the bird in the net, Tamiko carried it gently in both hands, while Mik carried the handle of the net so it wouldn't drag on the ground. Corky walked on the other side of Tamiko so he could grab the bird if it should try to escape, and Petey trailed along behind everybody.

When Mrs. Whipple opened the door and saw the four of them standing there with a big wiggly net, Mik thought she would lose the glasses right off her forehead. She had a habit of pushing them up there when she wasn't sewing or reading, but when she was surprised, her eyebrows would move upward, and then the glasses would fall right down on her nose. That was exactly what they did now. They fell on her nose with a soft little *clunk.*

"Goodness, what have you got there?" she asked, peering at the net. "What on earth is inside?"

They all talked at once, trying to tell her exactly what had happened. Petey began to jump up and down, he was so excited.

"And you say you found it in the park?" Mrs. Whipple asked. "Do you suppose it is really Mr. Potts's pheasant?"

"Must be," Mik said. "There can't be that many ring-necked pheasants running around Berkeley."

"You're right, Mikitaro," Mrs. Whipple said. "I do believe you're right. But there's one way to find out for sure."

She hurried to her closet and put on her coat and hat. She never went calling without them, and if she weren't just going next door, she would even have taken her gloves.

"Now," she said. "Let's go. I am very interested to know what Mr. Potts will have to say to this."

They looked like a small army about to attack a fortress. Petey rang the bell. It was a friendly sounding *bing-bong*, not at all the kind of bell one would expect at the house of an ogre like Mr. Potts.

They heard Mr. Potts shuffle to the door, and the moment he opened it, Mik shouted, "We found your bird! We found your ring-necked pheasant!"

Before Mr. Potts could say a word, they all pushed their way into his house, wet squishy shoes and all. Tamiko knelt on the floor, opened her net, and let the pheasant out. It tumbled out with a rustle of its wings and went at once to peck at Mr. Potts's shoe.

"Why, it *is* my Mathilda!" Mr. Potts said, taking her up in his arms. "But where . . . how . . . what happened?"

Mik and Corky and Tamiko told their story once more, and as they talked, Mrs. Whipple stood there, nodding her head.

"Imagine," she murmured. "Bless my soul! Fancy that!"

When they had finished, she faced Mr. Potts squarely. "This does prove once and for all that Cassandra and Fredericka didn't eat your birds, doesn't it?" she asked.

Mr. Potts cleared his throat noisily. "Well," he began, "what about my parakeets?" He made a feeble attempt to argue, but everyone could see that he didn't really want to.

"You won't do anything to Cass or Freddie now, will you?" Mik asked. "This proves they didn't eat your birds, doesn't it?"

Mr. Potts cleared his throat once more. "Well, at least they didn't eat the pheasant." He looked as though he wanted to admit he was wrong, but he had never in the world admitted anything like that. He had never said he was sorry to anyone, and he wasn't going to begin now.

"I . . . that is . . . well . . ." he began, and then he turned suddenly and hobbled off toward the kitchen. When he came back, he was carrying Carmichael's cage.

"Here," he said, thrusting it at Mik. "One good bird deserves another. Since you have returned a bird to me, I'll return yours."

Mik thought he was dreaming. "You mean you're giving Carmichael back?" he asked. "You really are?"

"You aren't going to keep him, then?" Corky asked, amazed.

"I couldn't take your pet away from you," Mr. Potts said slowly. "I know what a pet can mean."

It was just as Mr. Monroney had said. Mik did get back his pet parrot. Petey put away the water pistol he had been pointing at Mr. Potts.

"You're not so mean, after all," Tamiko said with a grin.

And if Mrs. Whipple had known Mr. Potts a little better, she probably would have gone up to him and given him an enormous hug. "Why, Mr. Potts," she said, beaming, "you do have a heart, after all. I thought maybe you did, somewhere beneath all that grouchiness."

Mr. Potts wasn't sure whether to be flattered at being told he had a heart, or insulted at being called a grouch. He was embarrassed to have everyone staring at him as though he had two heads.

"I taught Carmichael how to whistle," he said suddenly.

"You did?" Mik asked. "How?"

"Well, it takes patience," Mr. Potts began. "I spent a lot of time with him, so he would get to know and trust me. Then I began to whistle a short tune. He listened and I whistled. I whistled every time I came to his cage, and one day he copied me. He had learned to whistle."

Mr. Potts was talking to them like an old friend. "You could have done it with a little more time," he said to Mik.

"You Carmichael's friend?" Petey asked Mr. Potts.

Mr. Potts looked embarrassed. "I believe so," he said, hesitating.

"Then you must be Mik's friend, too," Tamiko said.

Mrs. Whipple knew when to step in. "Of course he is," she said, so Mr. Potts would not have the burden of the answer.

"We are all friends now," she said, and she thrust her hand toward Mr. Potts. "I forgive you for having blamed Cassie and Freddie and Mikitaro," she said grandly. "You were wrong, but I'm sure you are sorry."

She said all the words so Mr. Potts wouldn't have to speak them.

He stood looking down at the floor, but he did not deny her words. "It is good to have friends again," he said in a low voice.

Mik felt as though he should say something nice. "You taught Carmichael how to whistle," he said.

"And I caught your pheasant," Tamiko said, as though no one knew. "I caught your ring-necked pheasant."

If it hadn't been for Tamiko and her big net, they certainly wouldn't have the pheasant now, and Mr. Potts would never have admitted that the cats were innocent. Maybe, Mik thought, he would never have gotten Carmichael back either.

"I guess that old net was a pretty good thing after all," he admitted.

Tamiko scratched the tip of her nose. "Sure it was," she said, grinning. "I told you I would catch something wonderful in it someday."

Corky felt he should say something nice, too. "Guess it was a good thing you came from Japan," he said solemnly.

"Sure," Tamiko said, nodding.

"Sure," Petey agreed.

And Mik found himself grinning back at Tamiko. She wasn't so bad, after all.

CHAPTER 11

Mr. Monroney Tells

Mr. Potts was no longer an enemy, and Cass and Freddie were safe, but there was one more problem left to solve. Who was the prowler, and what did Mr. Monroney know about him?

Mik decided there was only one way to find out, and that was to come right out and ask Mr. Monroney. It wasn't until Sunday afternoon, however, that he had his chance.

Everybody was sitting under the peach tree in the back yard, having pink lemonade. Dad and Bud were listening to the Giants game on the radio, Mom was reading the paper, Petey was digging a hole just to see how deep he could dig, and Tamiko was sitting with the net on her lap, waiting to catch a butterfly. Bowser was having a nap in the sun, and Carmichael was back in his usual spot beside the kitchen window.

Mik was the only one who couldn't sit still. He kept jumping up and running around to the front of the house to watch for Mr. Monroney. When he jumped up for about the tenth time, he heard the bells of the ice-cream cart at last. He saw Mr. Monroney in his starched white jacket, jingling his bells. He was looking up at the sky as he walked, as though a customer might come flying down to him from up there.

"Whatcha looking up there for?" Mik asked.

Mr. Monroney grinned. "Just checking the cloud formations," he said. Mr. Monroney knew a great deal about the sky and the clouds. He could usually tell what the weather would be like just by watching the sky.

"Looks like clear weather ahead," he said.

But Mik couldn't be bothered with the weather. "I got Carmichael back, and we found Mr. Potts's pheasant," he said, spilling out all the good news at once. He'd waited a long time to tell Mr. Monroney. He hadn't been around at all during the rainy weather.

"So I hear, so I hear," Mr. Monroney said. Mr. Monroney usually heard the news almost as soon as it had happened.

"I told you you'd be getting Carmichael back someday, didn't I?" Mr. Monroney asked, looking pleased.

Mik nodded. "How'd you know?" he asked.

"I know many things," Mr. Monroney answered mysteriously.

"Like who the prowler is?" Mik asked.

Mr. Monroney didn't answer that question. Instead he asked one of his own. "How is everybody? All right?"

"They're fine. They're drinking lemonade," Mik explained. "Want some?"

Now, Mr. Monroney never refused a glass of lemonade, not even on a cold, snowy day. It was his favorite drink. So, of course, on a nice warm 75-degree day, he certainly wasn't going to say no. He parked his cart, took his hat (he was taking no more chances of its being stolen), and followed Mik into the back yard.

When he appeared, everybody welcomed him as though he were Santa Claus himself.

"Well, Mr. Monroney, have a chair," Dad said, getting up to offer his own.

"Listen to the game with us," Bud offered.

"How about a glass of lemonade?" Mom asked.

"Gimme 'nother ride," Pete demanded.

Mr. Monroney answered everybody but Pete, whom he tried hard to ignore. He wanted no part of any more wild hair-raising rides. He did sit down and listen to the game, however.

Mik waited until he had finished half of his lemonade, and then he asked, "Mr. Monroney, tell us who the prowler is."

Mr. Monroney pretended to be listening to the game. He acted as though he hadn't heard. But Dad heard. He turned and looked at Mr. Monroney.

"You know," he said, "that still puzzles me, too. Do you know something that we don't know?"

Mr. Monroney pulled at his mustache. "Well, yes," he said

slowly. "I've known for some time now, but I was hoping he would go tell Mr. Potts and Mrs. Whipple himself. I was hoping I wouldn't have to be the one to tell."

No one was listening to the game any more.

"Who was it, for heaven's sake?" Mom asked.

"Yeah, Mr. Monroney, tell us," Mik urged.

Mr. Monroney looked troubled and wiggled his toe uncomfortably. Tamiko flapped her net at a passing butterfly, but missed. She sat down beside Mr. Monroney and pulled Pete onto her lap. Everyone was waiting, and Mr. Monroney could no longer remain silent.

"I don't like to be the bearer of tales," he said, still hesitating, "but, well . . . it was Mr. Potts's nephew. He broke into Mrs. Whipple's house, and he is also the one who opened the aviary and let the birds go."

"Mr. Potts's nephew!" everyone exclaimed.

"Why, I didn't know he had any relatives at all," Dad said.

Mr. Monroney nodded. "Oh, yes. He has tried hard to ignore them, but he has a brother-in-law and a nephew. The brother-in-law is an invalid, and the nephew—well, he's gotten into all sorts of trouble. I suppose it's mainly from growing up without a mother. He's had to do most of the housework and the cooking for the two of them. Some days he probably just didn't bother to get enough to eat."

"Imagine a growing boy like that going hungry!" Mother said.

"I've given him ice-cream bars from time to time," Mr.

Monroney went on, "and so he confided in me. He considers me a friend. That's why I didn't want to tell."

Mik began to put all the pieces together. And to think it was Mr. Potts's own nephew!

"And who is this nephew?" Dad asked.

"Anybody we know?" Mik asked. "Tell us, Mr. Monroney."

Mr. Monroney pulled at the words now, as though he didn't want to let them out.

"He's a proud youngster. I believe you know him, Mik. His name is Clancy. Clancy Berryman."

"Clancy Berryman!" Mik shouted, and he slid right off his chair and sprawled out on the grass.

CHAPTER 12

Mik, A Real Prince

Now, at the very moment that Mr. Monroney was talking to the Watanabes about the prowler, Mr. Potts himself was doing some serious thinking. He was standing outside in his garden, looking at Mathilda and pondering all the events that had brought her back to him.

It was a miracle that she was ever found—a miracle brought about by Mik Watanabe and a little girl with a big net from Japan. But Mr. Potts knew deep inside that the real miracle came even before that. It started when Mik brought him his pet parrot, Carmichael. At that moment Mr. Potts felt something he had never felt before. He understood that Mik had cared enough about Cassandra and Fredericka and Mrs. Whipple to give up his very own pet for them. He had also been generous enough to give this pet to him, a grouchy, cranky, unreasonable old man.

Mr. Potts had felt then that the things he had done and said in anger and misunderstanding were wrong—very wrong. Since he had had a chance to make things right again by returning Carmichael, it was amazing how much better he felt. It was so much easier to be friendly and pleasant than to be cross and irritable. Now he could go outside and look over at Mrs. Whipple's yard without scowling like an old scarecrow trying to frighten away the birds. That was exactly what he had been all these years, a scarecrow, frightening away all his friends.

As Mr. Potts stood there gazing at Mathilda, he decided it was time for him to do something good and kind for a change. He decided to begin by calling on his brother-in-law and his nephew Clancy. He had been very unsympathetic to Clancy the last time he came to borrow some money. In fact, he had simply scowled and sent the boy off without a cent. Mr. Potts didn't have a great deal of money, but he had more than the Berrymans. He stuffed twenty-five dollars in his wallet, combed the few strands of hair on top of his head, and set out for Clancy's house.

When he arrived, there was a smile on his face, and when Clancy opened the door, Mr. Potts held out his hand to him.

"I've come to tell you that I shall try to be a better uncle," he said simply.

Clancy looked at him suspiciously. "Are you sick or something?" he asked.

But Mr. Potts did not get angry. He simply laughed. "Sit down, boy, sit down," he said, and he had a long talk with Clancy and his father.

When he had finished, Clancy looked down at his toes,

and he confessed that he had let the birds go. "I wouldn't have done it if I hadn't been so mad and hungry," he said. "I wanted to get even with you for not helping us out."

Even then Mr. Potts's anger did not return. "I'm afraid I deserved it," he said. "It was my own fault."

When at last he was ready to leave, Mr. Potts urged Clancy to come with him. "The next person we must talk to is Mrs. Whipple," he said.

And that was how Clancy and Mr. Potts happened to be standing on Mrs. Whipple's porch. It just so happened that Mr. Monroney came by at that very moment, having rested and refreshed himself with lemonade at the Watanabes. When he saw Clancy and Mr. Potts standing together on Mrs. Whipple's porch, he knew that all was well. He waved his good-luck hat at Clancy and went on down the street. He was right to have kept quiet. He had known that Clancy would tell when the right time came, and it looked as though Clancy had told at last.

Mr. Monroney felt good. He felt extraordinarily good. He jingled his bells noisily and walked briskly up the street, whistling a tune. And his hat was on top of the cart, as it should be.

Mrs. Whipple had become quite used to surprises by this time. She had been told that a prowler had crawled in her window and eaten her food. She had had children come crowding in with a pheasant trapped in a net. Nothing can surprise me any more, she thought, as she went to the door. But when she saw Clancy Berryman and Mr. Potts standing there together, the glasses on her forehead plopped right down on her nose again—*clunk!*

"Why, Mr. Potts," she said, "and Clancy! Do come in."

Mrs. Whipple learned many things that afternoon. She learned that Clancy was Mr. Potts's nephew, and she learned that he was the prowler and that he had also unlocked Mr. Potts's aviary. She learned, too, why he did all these things.

"Oh, oh, my," she said as she listened. "My goodness. My goodness gracious. And you were hungry all the time," she said, turning to Clancy.

She hurried into the kitchen and brought out two enormous slices of pineapple upside-down cake. "I had a feeling I would have callers today," she explained. "Now sit right there while I make some tea."

She made Clancy eat two pieces of cake and drink two glasses of milk.

"And the next time you're hungry," she said, "you ring my doorbell and walk in. No more climbing in while I'm away!"

Clancy promised that he would, and Mrs. Whipple, feeling full of warm, friendly thoughts, invited him then and there to come to dinner the following Sunday.

"Bring your father if he's well enough to come," she instructed. And then she turned to Mr. Potts. "You come, too," she said.

It was the first time in twenty years that anyone had invited Mr. Potts to dinner. And it was the first time in almost as many years that Mr. Potts had said thank you to anyone.

Mrs. Whipple never felt better than when she was planning all sorts of spicy, stewy concoctions to put inside hungry people. Already she began to plan a menu full of nice nourishing dishes, and when Clancy and Mr. Potts went home, their mouths were watering at the mere thought of Sunday.

Mrs. Whipple then put on her Sunday coat and hat, and she took her bag and gloves too, because she was going farther than just next door. In fact, she was going to call on the Watanabes. She filled a big cake box with almond crescents, gingersnaps, macaroons, and butter crunches from her cooky jar and then set out with the box in her hand and a smile on her face.

When she arrived at the Watanabes', she looked as though she wanted to hug every one of them, but especially Mik. Mik could tell. He stayed a safe distance away as Mrs. Whipple told them what had just happened.

"So now we know who the prowler was, and we are all good friends," she explained happily. "Even Mr. Potts and Clancy."

But I'm not Clancy's friend, Mik thought. Clancy was still a mean ogre as far as he was concerned. It was Clancy's fault, after all, that Mik had had so much trouble with Mr. Potts.

Mrs. Whipple seemed to know exactly what he was thinking. "Clancy is really a good boy," she said. "He simply hasn't had a chance, being without a mother and all."

"Imagine his having to take care of himself and his father all alone," Mik's mother said. "It makes me want to cry."

But Mik didn't feel like crying for Clancy.

"And having a father who is sick and can't work," Dad went on. "The poor fellow needs a break."

"Mr. Monroney said that's why he stole his hat," Bud added. "Clancy just wanted to have some good luck for a change."

Well, Mik knew Clancy was an ogre even if no one else did. "He took money from the little guys at the State Fair so he could buy extra hot dogs," he reminded them.

"Because he was hungry, probably," Tamiko said gently.

"He needs friends, Mik," Dad said. "Just like Mr. Potts, he needs a little kindness to bring out the good in him."

Mik heard, but he didn't say anything.

Mom suddenly brightened. She'd had one of her ideas. "Wouldn't it be wonderful if he could go to summer camp with the boys?" she asked.

Mrs. Whipple said she was sure he had never been to summer camp before.

Mik sat without saying a word. He was thinking now about the camp fund they had made for Tamio Mihara. Everyone had forgotten about it since Tamiko had turned out to be a girl. But it was still there. Mik knew that, and he knew, too, that it hadn't been promised to anyone else. He wondered if he was the only one who remembered it. He sat slouched in the big chair, half lying, half sitting, and thinking very hard. He thought for a long while, and then he spoke up.

"I guess Clancy could have that camp fund we have at church," he said. "Tamiko can't go to YMCA camp."

Everybody turned and beamed at Mik as though he had brought home a straight-A report card and been elected president of the school.

"Why, Mik, that's a wonderful idea," Mom said happily.

"With that for a start, Mr. Potts would surely help get him to camp," Dad said enthusiastically.

"In fact, I could sell more soap for him if there's time," Bud volunteered. "I've got lots of prospects," he added, looking slightly smug.

Maybe it wouldn't be *that* bad having Clancy at camp, Mik thought. After all, he'd been able to stand having a girl in the house for almost a month, and in the end she hadn't turned out to be bad at all.

"There, you see, Mikitaro," Mrs. Whipple said to him. "Everything has turned out beautifully, and it's all because you did such a fine job." She looked as though she wanted to hug him.

"You did much more, you know, than just take care of my garden and the cats," she went on. "You did something quite wonderful for Mr. Potts and for Clancy."

"And for yourself, too," Dad added. "If anybody asked, I think maybe I'd say you were a real prince, Mik!"

"On a golden charger!" Mom added, smiling.

Mik grinned. He did feel pretty good, at that. In fact, he felt as though he could even turn into a very responsible fellow someday.